Velvet's Wings

Written by Luke Alistar

Illustrated by Stephen Lauser

Luke Alistar

ISBN: 978-1480146204
First edition

Cover art and illustrations by Stephen Lauser

For Phoebe, Naomi, Joseph, Mary, Charity,
and Christina

My little brother and all my little sisters who were
too young to read my other books

Chapter 1

Stuck in a Mailbox

A dark cell. A locked door. They left her there, left her to die. She was bleeding, crying, stripped of her spirit and her glory like a condemned criminal.

But she can't remember why.

She didn't know her name. She didn't know where she was, or how she got there. All she knew was pain. It was dark, and something heavy held her against a wall of rough material. She couldn't see what it was because it was too dark. She groaned and whimpered and shoved the object. It moved a little and she managed to get free.

But she was in a box. The walls felt slightly fuzzy but hard. Like paper. How did she remember what paper was? She didn't know.

The box wasn't high enough for her to stand up. She stood hunched over and felt along the wall until she came to the corner. Her prison was about long enough for her to lie down in, and just as wide. It was half as tall as her.

In one of the walls she felt a hole covered in a tough, sticky material. The hole was big enough for her to crawl through, if only it wasn't plugged by the sticky stuff. She felt around, found something thin, and ran her hands over it. Whatever it was, she didn't know, but when she stabbed it into the sticky stuff, she was able to cut a hole.

It was just as dark outside the box as inside. When she climbed through she landed on a hard, cold surface and collapsed. Her chest still felt crushed, and a terrible pain stabbed through her middle. She crawled a short distance until she hit her head on a wall that felt the same as the floor. It was metal. She escaped the paper box only to be stuck in a metal one.

She leaned against the cold wall, breathing heavily. The pain was terrible, and her head pounded.

For a long time she slumped there, drifting in and out of consciousness. And then she was startled and nearly scared to death by a loud bang and a flood of blinding light. One end of the metal box had opened.

A giant hand reached in and grabbed the paper box, along with some large sheets of paper. She huddled in the corner, not wanting to be shut up again but deathly afraid of being seen by...whatever that was.

Then the face appeared. Each eye was nearly as big as her head. The teeth were the size of her hands. When it saw her, the eyes got bigger and the mouth dropped open.

"Please," she whimpered. "Please don't hurt me."

The giant hand reached in, right for her. She flinched and curled up, certain that she was about to be crushed or eaten. But the fingers wrapped gently around her and drew her out of the metal box.

Then the giant spoke. "What in the world are you?"

The voice was a boy's, somehow she knew that. A young boy. But...he was at least five times taller than her.

What was she? Good question. "I don't know," she cried. "Please don't hurt me."

"How did you...I must be dreaming! You're a tiny little person and you were in my mailbox."

She just whimpered. "Please don't hurt me."

The boy looked around and then back at her. "Don't be afraid. I won't hurt you. I'm not like other boys who like to squash and poke little living things. Do you have a name?"

She shook her head. "Maybe. I don't know."

"How'd you get in the mailbox? If I'm not dreaming, that is."

She trembled. "I don't know! I don't remember anything."

The boy nodded with a wise look. "Amnesia," he said. "I heard about it from a movie."

"What's it mean?"

"That you can't remember things. Which is too bad. I'd like to know how you got so small."

She twisted in his hand. He probably thought he was holding her gently, but every twitch of his fingers sent a jolt of fear through her, and made her sore body hurt worse.

"Don't worry," the boy said. "I'll take care of you."

Then he tucked her in his huge coat pocket and told her to curl up. She did, quaking so much that he warned her to keep still.

The pocket swayed back and forth and she began to feel sick, but before long he took her out and set her on a wooden surface.

"This is my room," he said.

She looked around at the huge place, turning in a complete circle. Posters of airplanes and helicopters and other aircraft covered three of the walls. The other held a large fabric thing that was draped over hooks like a curtain and trailed thin ropes.

"That's a parachute my Dad and I made a couple years ago," the boy said. "I spent a week with him and we did all sorts of crazy things." He sat down in a chair and watched her.

He'd put her on his desk, and there was a mirror by the wall. She stared at it.

"Do you even know what you look like?" the boy asked. He grabbed the mirror and moved it closer to her. The reflection pitched and streaked by crazily, making her feel sick until a version of herself stood almost motionless facing her.

Her brown hair hung just past her chin, almost straight but tangled and dirty. Her eyes were green, a very bright green that would make grass look dull, and they were set in a perfectly symmetrical, lightly freckled face with soft pink lips. She wore a blue jacket over a pink shirt, and dark blue pants. There were tiny sneakers on her feet.

The boy took a ruler and stood it up beside her. It was just as tall as her, and she stared at the reflected numbers.

"Twelve inches," the boy said, keeping his wide stare on her. "How does a person get twelve inches tall?"

She sank to her knees and covered her face with her hands and sobbed. It was so frightening, not knowing anything about herself.

A finger bigger than her arm gently touched her head. She looked up and saw a sad look on the boy's face.

"You don't need to cry," he said.

She sat down with her legs crossed and rubbed her eyes. "What if I'm not tiny?" she asked. "Maybe you're just really big."

"Nah. I've seen hundreds and thousands of people my size, and only one your size."

She sighed. It was a silly idea anyway.

"Don't feel bad. Well, I guess you're stuck with me for a while. I'm Jason, but people call me Jase."

"I don't know my name," she muttered.

"Then I'll give you one."

She looked up and watched as Jase climbed onto his bed and took down a stack of books from a shelf. He set them on the desk and opened one, careful not to hit her with it.

"There should be a good name in here," he said. "This is one of my favorite books."

At the top of all the right-hand pages she saw the title *Through the Dragon's Eyes*. Jase flipped through the book, sending up a lot of dust. He didn't seem to notice, but the particles swarmed around her like distracting insects.

"Here we go," he said. "Tierza. That's a nice name, isn't it?"

She nodded. It sounded good.

"Awesome." He closed that book and opened a thicker one. "There's a faerie in this one. She's three inches tall and has wings."

The title this time read *Circle of Three*.

"What's the faerie's name?" she asked.

Jase pointed to a spot on the page. "Velvet. How's that? A first name and a last name."

"What?"

"Tierza Velvet. You like it?"

"Yes, I guess so."

Jase put the books aside and sat down again, leaning his elbows on the desk. "I wonder how old you are," he said.

She was still trying on her new name. She imagined it would feel awkward for a while, like a new pair of shoes.

"Tierza?"

She blinked. "What?"

"I'm eleven. But how old are you?"

"What do you think?"

"You look as old as my sister, and she's seventeen."

Tierza shrugged. "It doesn't matter."

"I guess not. No matter how old you are, Mom probably won't let me keep you."

She looked up suddenly, frightened by his words in a way she couldn't figure out.

"Oh, don't worry. I'll hide you. It should be fine. If it's too dangerous in here then I have a treehouse where you could live."

Tierza stared out the window, at the huge world, the cars and trees and dogs and people, all so much bigger than her. How did a person get so small?

"You know what," Jase said. "You remind me of some fun books about little people. They were about half as tall as you."

"What were they called?"

"Borrowers, because they went around and borrowed things from the humans."

Tierza stared at her hands and bent her fingers. "I'm not human?"

Jase didn't answer. He looked confused.

"It's okay," she sighed. "I don't really care what I am. I mean, I want to know, but it doesn't really make any difference."

"Okay. But aren't you afraid that scientists will want to experiment on you? If you're not human they won't worry about doing all sorts of mean things."

"Then don't let them!"

Jase hunched over and rested his chin on his arms. "I'm just a kid though. I think you'll be safe, but if someone finds you, they could take you away."

Just then a loud knock came from the door. "Jason!" a voice called. "Open your door this instant!"

"Uh oh," he hissed. "I think the cookie police just caught up with me."

He snatched her off the desk before she could react and set her under the bed. "Stay hidden," he said.

Tierza peered out as Jase opened the door. A woman stood there, towering over the boy with a scowl.

"Sorry, Mom," Jase said. "But you left the cookies out on the counter. I thought they were up for grabs."

The woman shook her head, but there was a trace of a smile on her lips. "You should know better than that." Then she looked past him into the room. "Were you talking to someone in here?"

"Who, me? Oh, no, the army men and I were just discussing battle strategies."

"I see. Well, come with me. I have some work for you to do in payment for those cookies."

Jase glanced back at the bed, and held out one hand as if motioning for Tierza to stay. "Hold your positions," he said in a commanding voice. "I'll be back shortly."

Then he left and the door slammed shut behind him.

Tierza wrapped her arms around the metal leg of the bed and stared at the door for a long time.

Chapter Two

Pain and Fear

When Jase returned a couple hours later, he brought with him a stack of books. He dropped them on the bed and looked around. Then under the bed. Then he sat down.

"Tierza, are you here? Sorry I was gone so long. Mom took me to the library with her."

She watched him from behind the desk. Being left alone in this strange, huge place for so long had frightened her, and when painful cramps attacked her chest, she crawled into the dark space to hide. Now she had to work up the courage to leave her hiding place.

Jase smiled when he saw her. "There you are! I was almost afraid I went crazy and you didn't actually exist."

He reached down and picked her up, and set her on the bed. She tripped on the folds of the blanket and fell over.

"Sorry. Look what I got."

He held up a book titled *Faeries, Sprites, and Leprechauns: Everything You Never Knew About The Fay.*

"Found it at the library," he said as he flipped through it. "And I think it's rubbish. Interesting, but it's all about magic and myths and legends. There's no recent research on faeries."

Tierza curled her legs in and rested her elbows on her knees. "I'm hungry," she said.

Jase looked up from his book. "What?"

"I said I'm...hungry."

He made a thoughtful face and looked back at the book. "Perfect. It says here that faeries like to eat mostly flower leaves. We can test that, do our own research. I'll be right back."

He dropped the book beside her and she flinched as he raced out of the room. Her vision flashed bright and she gasped.

Pain. Of beating and betrayal. She was falling, but nobody caught her. Someone tried to kill her...

A bright light and warmth. Using the last of her strength to crawl into a shelter. Then darkness. More pain.

"Tierza?"

She blinked and saw Jase standing there. She was curled up, hugging her knees to her chest and shuddering.

"Are you scared?"

Tierza closed her eyes and cried. She wasn't quite sure why. It was a sorrow of being lost and alone, but she was safe for now. Maybe there was too much emptiness inside her and she had to let it out.

"Here...why don't you try eating?"

Something brushed her head and she looked up at the rose petal. Jase tore off a piece and handed it to her, and she took a bite and chewed.

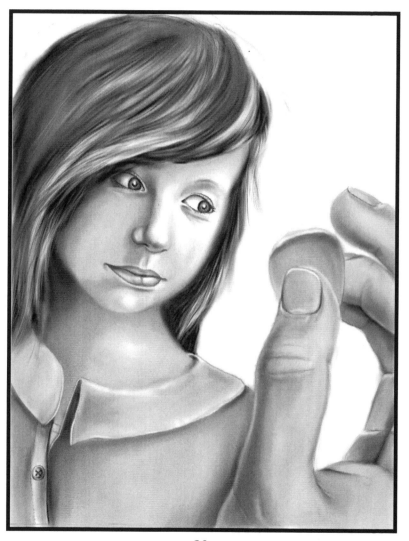

"Well, how is it?" he asked, sitting down and making the bed tilt.

She shrugged and swallowed. "It's okay."

"Maybe it'll help you remember things." He handed her another piece.

Tierza didn't think so, but the first bite had kindled her hunger and she kept eating until she was full.

"Feel better now?" Jase asked, looking up from his book.

"I guess."

"I think I know why you're sad. You have a home somewhere and you probably miss it, even if you can't remember it."

Tierza shuddered, remembering her disturbing flashback. "I don't know. I think I don't have a home anymore."

He set the book down and stretched out on the bed on his side, his face about a foot away from her. "Did you remember something?"

"No," she lied. Really, she had no idea what she remembered. Just a lot of pain.

"You know what, maybe instead of figuring out what you are, we should figure out where you came from first." He sat up suddenly. "Do you have any idea how you ended up in the mailbox?"

Tierza pointed at the box on his desk. "I woke up in that and crawled out. But I still don't remember anything."

Jase went to the desk, paused, and then came back and brought her with him. He set her by the mirror and opened the box.

"It's some art supplies I ordered," he said, taking out a handful of colored pencils. "You must have used this to get out." He held up a small pair of scissors.

She shrugged.

Jase emptied the box and then folded the flaps down. He looked at the label. "It came from San Francisco. We're in Fresno. Somehow we need to find out where this box was sealed up. You had to have gotten into it before that."

Just then, the door burst open and Jase turned, leaning over the desk to hide Tierza. She crouched by his arm, trembling. Sharp pain stabbed through her middle and she pressed her hands to her chest as tears stung her eyes.

"Jason, did you tear apart one of my roses?"

It wasn't the boy's mother. This must be the sister he mentioned. Tierza leaned on his arm and tried to massage out the painful cramp in her chest.

Jase hesitated. "Uh...yes..."

"Why? Is there any good reason for that?"

"I'm sorry, Nikka. I just needed the petals."

"For?"

"I can't tell you."

Tierza heard the door close and she tensed.

"Of course you can tell me," Nikka said with a slight tone of annoyance.

"Well, you can't tell anyone else."

"I'm no blabbermouth."

"You promise?"

Nikka sighed. "If it wouldn't hurt anything, of course I won't tell."

"Okay..."

Tierza panicked and started to run, but she ran right into the mirror and fell down dazed. Jase picked her up tenderly and cradled her in his hands.

Nikka gasped and came closer. Tierza shook her head and blinked, trying to clear her vision.

"What is it?" Nikka asked.

"She," Jase asserted. "I named her Tierza Velvet because she can't remember anything. We're trying to figure out what she is and where she came from."

Nikka reached out and lightly touched the front of Tierza's blue jacket. "I hope you haven't been hurting her."

"Of course not!" Jase exclaimed in an indignant tone. "Tell her, Tierza."

The little girl shook her head. "Jase is nice."

At the sound of her voice, Nikka's eyes got wider, but she didn't say anything.

"She came out of my box of new art supplies," Jase said. "I found her locked in the mailbox."

"You should tell Mom about this," Nikka said, still staring at Tierza.

"Why? Mom might not let her stay."

Nikka swatted her brother's head. "Don't be silly. Mom's smart enough to know when someone needs help. She won't turn them away just because they're...tiny."

Jase looked doubtful. "Really?"

"Just try her. I'll back you up."

The boy shrugged and set Tierza on the desk. "I guess..."

The little girl got to her feet and limped over to the box, leaning against it and trying to catch her breath. The cramps in her belly hadn't gone away. They were getting worse.

Nikka knelt down with a concerned look. "Jase, she's hurt. Are you sure you didn't do anything?"

He shook his head. "Nothing, honest! She told you. I think she was already hurt when I found her."

Tierza nodded and collapsed to her knees. Her head spun and she couldn't seem to breathe right.

"She needs help," Nikka said, standing up. "What did you say you named her?"

"Tierza Velvet."

"Okay. Bring her and let's find Mom."

Jase scooped up Tierza and they left the room. Their mother was in the kitchen, putting a pizza in the oven. Jase let his sister go first and hung back behind her.

"Mom, there's something you need to see," Nikka said. She pulled Jase forward and he held out Tierza.

Mom closed the oven and turned around. "What is it this time...oh my word, what is *this?*"

Tierza flinched and hung onto Jase's thumb.

"I named her Tierza Velvet," the boy said. "I found her in the mailbox this morning. She can't remember anything."

Mom stared, as if trying to comprehend a twelve-inch-tall person and failing.

"I won't cause trouble," Tierza said, her voice quaking.

At that Mom smiled, though she still seemed a little thunderstruck.

"She's hurt," Nikka said.

"Then...get the first aid kit and we'll see if we can help. T...Tierza, what in the world are you?"

Jase frowned. "Don't hurt her feelings, Mom."

"You'll have to forgive me. It's not every day that my son comes into the kitchen with a new friend who's so...small. Much less a girl."

"Mom!"

Nikka returned with the first aid kit and Jase set Tierza on a folded towel on the counter. She lay there and stared up at them, her little heart racing. They seemed nice enough, but if they decided to do something—anything—she couldn't stop them. Knowing she was powerless only scared her more.

"Where does it hurt?" Mom asked.

Tierza patted her middle.

"Can you take off your jacket?"

The little girl sat up and unzipped the coat and pulled it off. Then she stared down at her feet and rubbed her hands on her pink shirt.

"Hmm," Mom said. "Jase, go arrange a place for Tierza to sleep."

"Where?"

"A shelf in your bedroom is fine."

When Jase left, Mom had Tierza lift her little pink shirt. The woman looked and grimaced.

"A lot of bruising," she said.

Tierza felt dizzy, and she flopped back as a tremendous pain sliced through her chest. She let out a moan.

"This looks serious," Mom said. "I would take you to the hospital..."

"No Mom, not the hospital!" Jase hollered from his room. "They'll want to experiment on her!"

"It wouldn't work anyway," Mom said. "Their tools are too big. Nikka, call Miss Lindon."

"Who?"

"She's the one who fixed up the oriole that flew into the window last year."

"The bird lady?" Jase asked, coming into the room as Nikka left. "What could she do?"

"She has tiny instruments and a delicate touch."

"But Tierza isn't a bird."

"I'm sure Miss Lindon can figure that out."

"You'll have to swear her to secrecy."

Mom chuckled absently and stared at Tierza. The little girl smoothed out her shirt and shivered.

Chapter Three

She's a Person Too

"Good grief, Rayna, that isn't a bird!"

Tierza scooted backward across the counter as the young woman they called Miss Lindon peered at her through a pair of glasses.

"I know that," Mom said. "But can you help?"

Jase tried to pick the little girl up and in a panic she bit his finger.

"Ouch," he hissed under his breath, and he jerked his hands away.

Tierza ducked behind a bowl of fruit and doubled over, gasping for air. When someone moved the bowl, she collapsed and started crying.

"She's hurt," Jase said. "And scared. Be careful!"

Miss Lindon picked Tierza up in slender fingers, much gentler than Jase could. The little girl still struggled, beginning to feel faint with pain.

"I'll try to help," the woman said, "but I'll have to calm it down first."

"Not *it*," Jase snapped. "Her name is Tierza."

Miss Lindon looked at Rayna. "Haven't you talked to him about naming creatures prematurely?"

"Can't...breathe," Tierza gasped. Tears streamed down her cheeks and the pain in her middle almost paralyzed her.

"It talked!"

"She!" Jase shouted.

Miss Lindon laid Tierza on the folded towel. "I'm sorry. You're right. She does look human, just a lot smaller than usual. Has she been near any radioactive sludge recently?"

Their conversation faded away and Tierza drifted in and out of consciousness. Her fear gave way to complete panic, and all she could do was lie there and cry and feel those gentle fingers touching her.

"...has a broken rib, or two," she heard Miss Lindon say.

And then Jase's concerned voice. "Can you help?"

"Yes, but you'll have to make sure she rests for a while. I have no idea how fast it'll heal, but small things do tend to heal faster."

The fingers moved Tierza's shirt and felt all around her rib cage. She gasped at the cold touch, and it brought her back to consciousness, but she didn't have the strength to fight it.

"Amazing," Miss Lindon murmured. "Heart rate and body temperature are higher than ours, just like a bird, but the structure of the body seems to be biologically the same as a human."

"Lady, you aren't here to give me a science lesson," Jase said in a serious tone.

Miss Lindon only chuckled and lightly touched a spot on Tierza's chest that hurt a lot. "See these bruises? They're the worst, and if you look closely, you can see that the ribs underneath aren't as curved as the other side. That's where the break is. It's causing her trouble breathing by constricting the lung, and the pain when she inhales must be enormous."

"Uh huh, I see."

The fingers wrapped around Tierza, feeling for the right places, and then suddenly gave a sharp pinch. For a moment she lay frozen with pain, her mouth open wide. And then a full breath of air rushed into her lungs and she screamed.

"What did you do?" Jase demanded.

"Calm down," Miss Lindon said, unrolling some gauze strips. "I hardly did anything. Look at her. She's breathing just fine now. I got the bones straightened. Yes, it's very painful at first, but now they should heal correctly. Assuming she keeps still."

Tierza closed her eyes and sobbed as the pain subsided a little. The fingers wrapped bandages around her middle, just loose enough that she could breathe but tight enough to keep her stiff.

Miss Lindon pulled the little shirt down over Tierza's bandage. "There. Let her rest and I'll come back in a couple days with my portable x-ray machine."

Tierza opened her eyes and rubbed the tears out of them with her fists. Rayna and Nikka were still there, looking on with sympathetic expressions. Already the stabbing pain was bearable, and she kept sucking in deep breaths to feel how her lungs worked now.

"How is it?" Jase asked. "Better?"

She tried to sit up, but fell back with a sharp cry at a prick from the cracked ribs.

"Don't move," Miss Lindon said. "No sitting up or walking until I come back to check on you. Understand?"

Tierza nodded and relaxed, beginning to shiver again.

"Amazing," Miss Lindon muttered.

Jase reached for Tierza, but Nikka pushed his hands away. "I'll take her," she said.

The boy frowned, but Nikka was almost as gentle as Miss Lindon. She took the little girl into Jase's room and laid her on a small, fluffy blanket that was folded over a few times to make a small bed. A blue stuffed sea turtle made a comfortable pillow, and a handkerchief worked for a quilt.

"You heard Miss Lindon," Jase said. "Lie still and don't try to move around."

Tierza nodded, and Nikka smiled.

"What do you plan to do with the little thing?" Miss Lindon asked.

Rayna shrugged. "Jase has obviously claimed her, naming her and all. I don't mind keeping her here, at least for a little while."

"Someone should find out what she is and where she came from, though. I doubt she's...human."

"Why?"

"This isn't some freak of human biology. That creature is supposed to be that size. She's...well, perfect."

"Are you saying—"

"A new species, Rayna. Your son found a new apparently sentient species in your mailbox. This isn't something that can go unnoticed by science. This *Tierza* should be studied."

"I don't think she would like that."

"Does she have a choice?"

Rayna felt uncomfortable. "If she couldn't talk, that would be something else. But as far as I've seen, she's a real person."

"That depends on your definition of 'person.' Are you judging solely by the fact that she looks human and can communicate? Monkeys can be taught sign language, and many birds can be taught to speak English."

Perhaps, Rayna thought, but that was far different than speaking with intelligence. Tierza was plainly intelligent.

"Either way," Rayna said out loud, "if she's a person, she has the same rights as you and I do. If she's not, then she belongs to us, because we found her."

"It's your choice," Miss Lindon said, opening the door. "Just don't be selfish and keep the greatest scientific discovery of the millennium to yourself."

Rayna stared at the door as it closed behind the younger woman. Then she shook her head and rushed into the kitchen to check the pizza.

For the rest of the day, Jase and Nikka and their mother kept coming into the room to check on Tierza. She fell asleep after about half an hour, and woke up later that evening feeling starved.

Jase gave her a bit of his pizza crust, but she didn't like it. Pepperoni was even worse. Nikka brought her a piece of something called banana, and that was both delicious and filling. She also sacrificed another rose petal for the miniature girl, but Tierza decided she liked banana better.

They'd left her alone in the room for a while and she was beginning to get nervous when Jase came in and pulled his chair over to the shelf and climbed up on it.

"How are you feeling now?" he asked.

She tucked her hands behind her head. "Better," she said.

"Good. It's time for me to go to bed, but if you need anything in the night, just shout or make a beeping noise like an alarm clock. I'm a light sleeper."

"Okay."

"Tomorrow is Sunday, so we'll be going to church."

"Are there lots of people there?"

"Yes. Would that be too scary?"

Tierza nodded.

"I don't think we should leave you alone though. Hmm. I'll talk to Mom about that in the morning."

He got up and switched off the light. By the dim blue glow of a nightlight she saw him crawl into his bed.

"Goodnight, Tierza."

She watched him settle down. "Goodnight..."

After a few minutes Jase's breathing slowed and the house became very quiet. She closed her eyes, but she couldn't sleep.

A while passed and she began to shiver, so she pulled the blanket up tight around her neck. Then she looked at the window. Something moved in the darkness outside, and she stared, her heart racing.

A face pressed up against the window, large and glowing. The nose squashed against the glass and the eyes were fixed on Jase. Tierza started trembling, holding her breath and wondering if this was something out of her past coming to hurt her. But it looked a lot like Jase, except for the glowing.

She pulled the blanket over her face, hyperventilating, afraid that if she screamed the beast would see her—break in and steal her.

Chapter Four

Strange New Places

She scrambled under a small bush and crouched there, her breath coming in rapid, terrified bursts. Her heart raced so fast it was just a hum. Something was hunting her. She'd been turned away from her own home, and now they wanted to find her and hurt her.

She heard the sniffling of the tracking beast, and bolted out the other side of the bush with a strangled sob. An abrupt drop opened up in front of her and she tried to stop, but her momentum carried her over and she fell.

Tierza awoke with a jolt, covered in cold sweat. Sunlight streamed in through the window, and she remembered the glowing creature from the night before. Jase wasn't in the room, and she heard sounds from outside the door, which hung open a few inches.

She'd been dreaming about running and falling, but it seemed so real. Were they actual memories or simply concoctions of her damaged mind? Maybe the thing at the window had been her imagination too. Maybe she was simply going crazy.

Tierza tried sitting up, but the pain in her chest stopped her sharply. It wasn't as bad as it was yesterday, but it still hurt enough that she knew she should keep still. So she lay there and started shivering as her sweat evaporated.

"You're awake!" Jase exclaimed.

Tierza's heart jumped and she went rigid, wishing he could be quieter.

"Sorry, did I scare you?"

"Yes..."

"Anyway, Mom says that Nikka and I can stay home and take care of you. She's going to church and then visiting her friends later."

As he spoke, he cut up some pieces of banana and put them on a small plate for her.

"We're going to have so much fun," he continued. "Lots of fun today, because tomorrow Nikka and I have to go to school and Mom has to go to work."

Tierza nibbled on a piece of banana. "Will I be alone?"

"No, Miss Lindon will be coming by tomorrow morning and she'll take you with her for the day. Then

Mom will pick you up on the way home. It's all figured out."

She didn't say anything. It wasn't that she disliked Miss Lindon—after all, the woman had helped her. But Tierza had a hard time trusting anyone. Even Jase. They were all so much bigger, so her simple instincts made it hard for her to trust them.

"Jason, Nikka, I'm leaving now."

"Okay Mom!" Jase shouted. He turned to Tierza with a grin and then carefully picked her up, bed and all, and carried her out to the living room. He set her bed on the wide arm of the couch and plopped down on the cushion.

"Should we watch a movie?" he asked.

Nikka stepped into the room. "Not yet, Jase. You can do that later."

"Then what do we do right now?"

"Mom wanted us to read the Bible before we do anything else."

Jase leaned back. "Fine. Make it quick."

Nikka shook her head at him and sat down with a big, leather-bound book.

"Hey, we should see if we can find anything about faeries in the Bible," Jase suggested, suddenly leaning forward.

"I don't think there is."

"Lilliputians? Elves? Leprechauns? Pixies? Any little people at all?"

Nikka rolled her eyes. "Okay, a little person."

She opened the Bible, flipped through it, and then started reading in a lazy, paraphrased sort of way.

"And Jesus entered and went through Jericho, and there was a man named Zaccheus, who was the chief among the publicans—"

"Is that a race of tiny people?" Jase interrupted.

"No. They were the tax collectors."

"The tax collectors were tiny?"

Nikka huffed. "The publicans were tax collectors."

"Oh…"

"Anyway, Zaccheus was rich, probably because he was a sneaky thief. And he sought to see Jesus, but could not because of the crowd, because he was a short man."

"So the publicans *were* short people!"

"Just Zaccheus," Nikka said.

"Where does it say that?"

"Jase, just let me read the story."

"You're adding things to the Bible. That's hereticsy."

"Heresy, Jase, and no, it's not. The story is about Zaccheus, not *all* tax collectors! You're the one who wants to assume things."

The boy grumbled and slumped back on the couch. Nikka finished reading the story, and Jase declared that it was too deep and profound for his young mind to analyze, and then they put away the Bible and got out some games.

Tierza managed to sit up for a while, and she was glad to stretch out. Nikka was concerned that she would hurt herself more, but the bandages helped her keep her middle straight and stiff.

Jase taught her how to play checkers, and after a few games she beat him and he decided that was enough. She giggled as he muttered under his breath about being beaten by a twelve-inch girl.

They watched a movie that afternoon about a mad scientist who made a shrinking machine and accidentally shrunk his kids to just an inch or two tall.

Jase made loud comments throughout the movie and Nikka drifted in and out of the room, sometimes reading a book and sometimes snacking on chips or popcorn.

As the day wore on, Tierza felt more and more uncomfortable. They treated her well, but she still had a feeling that, to them, she was a different creature entirely. She wasn't a human shrunk down, and she felt out of place. A twelve-inch tall girl didn't belong here, and never would.

That night, as Jase lay down to sleep, she clutched the edge of her handkerchief quilt and watched the window. If the creature came back, she planned to wake up Jase so he could chase it off for good.

But it didn't show up, and eventually all the exhausting stress and fear caught up with her and she drifted off to sleep.

Tierza woke on Monday morning lying on her side. Her chest was still sore but better, and her cheeks were stiff with tears. She'd cried during the night, but now she couldn't remember what her dark dreams had been about.

With a whimper she rolled onto her back. Jase sat on the edge of the bed, pulling his socks on.

"Jase," Rayna called from somewhere else in the house, "bring the little...uh, bring Tierza out here. Miss Lindon is at the door."

The boy stood up and rubbed his eyes, then picked up Tierza's bed and carried her out of the room.

"Do I have to go?" she asked, her voice trembling.

"I don't think you want to go to school with me or Nikka," he muttered. "And Mom has to work."

Miss Lindon took her from Jase with those gentle hands and smiled. Even so, Tierza started hyperventilating. She was being taken away, out into the big world, and she wasn't ready to handle that. She wanted to stay, even if she'd be alone. But she couldn't seem to get the words out; they stuck in her throat and made it feel sore.

"Thank you," Miss Lindon said. "I'll take good care of her."

Rayna slipped past Jase and out the door, her keys dangling from one finger. "I'll drop by about five-fifteen to pick Tierza up."

Miss Lindon nodded and then headed for her car.

"You'd better take good care of her!" Jase shouted.

A giant yellow school bus stopped by the curb, its brakes squealing. Jase slung a backpack over his shoulder and ran for the bus, waving goodbye to Tierza.

She started waving back, and then saw the other boy coming from farther down the street. She only got a quick look at him before Miss Lindon opened her car door and set Tierza on the passenger seat. But a quick look was enough. She knew that face. And it made her tremble. He was the creature at the window.

"Don't look so frightened!" Miss Lindon said when she climbed into the driver's seat. "I'm a veterinarian. I make little creatures better, not worse. Speaking of which, how are the ribs feeling?"

Tierza pulled the blanket over her face and sulked.

"Fine then. You don't have to tell me. Not many of my patients can tell me how they feel anyway. I have other ways to find out."

Tierza shifted a little in the bed as the car moved. Miss Lindon hummed to herself during the drive, leaving the little girl alone with her thoughts. When the car stopped and the woman climbed out, Tierza pulled the handkerchief blanket off her face and looked around.

The hands picked her up with her bed and carried her into a house. There was a sign in the yard that read *Rachel Lindon's Animal Clinic*.

The front entrance was watched over by a plump young lady behind a desk. Miss Lindon pulled the handkerchief to cover Tierza's head as they went through the door.

"I thought you'd be gone longer, Rachel," an unfamiliar voice said. "What is that?"

"Just an injured bird," Miss Lindon said. "I have work to do for the rest of the morning, so if anyone comes in, send them to Doctor Kintz."

"Yes ma'am."

Tierza heard a door close and then the handkerchief was taken away. She turned onto her side and curled up, shivering. She still had her jacket, but the room was cold and her clothes weren't enough to keep in her tiny body's heat.

The gentle fingers lifted her off her bed, and Rachel's huge face loomed above her with a smile that Tierza didn't like. A victorious smile, one that said Rachel was in charge here and there was nothing the little girl could do about it.

There were cages all around the room, some empty, some occupied by small creatures. One held a cat that stood up and fixed its unblinking stare on Tierza. She shuddered and squirmed in the woman's hands, but those practiced fingers held her firmly.

"Let's see how the little creature is doing," Rachel said, laying Tierza on a tray and latching a clear plastic lid over her. "Just a few x-rays should show how the ribs are healing."

Chapter Five

The Cage

Tierza panicked as Rachel slid her into a dark metal box. She sat up, slamming her head into the clear plastic lid. She whimpered and rolled over and crawled until she hit a wall, and then turned and continued to the corner. There she stopped, lying facedown and breathing in jagged gasps. Her chest hurt a little, but the sharp pain of two days ago was gone. She could move on her own again just fine.

So why was she in this dark prison?

Tierza curled up there in the darkness and sobbed, waiting for a chance to get free. The fragmented memories that were beginning to come back were of things she'd rather not remember. If only she could get back to Jase and live without her memories, she might be happy.

After a time that may have been just a minute or two—or an hour, she couldn't tell—Rachel pulled her out of the dark place and set the tray on the counter. Tierza tensed and prepared to run as soon as the lid was lifted.

But Rachel was expecting that. She unlatched the plastic lid and opened it just far enough to reach her hand in. By the time Tierza realized what was happening, it was too late. Rachel flung the lid up and grabbed her with a gloved hand.

Tierza bit the hand, but her tiny teeth did nothing against the thick rubber glove. Rachel held her up.

"That's not very nice. And not humanlike at all. Good news though, your ribs are mostly healed. That was quite fast, even for a creature of your size."

Tierza could figure that much out herself from the fact that the pain in her chest was only a dull throb now.

"Now just calm down and it'll make things easier for both of us. I'm going to check a few things and take a blood sample, and I'd prefer to not have to restrain you."

Tierza said nothing, but went limp, hoping Rachel would take it as an answer.

She did. The woman set her on the folded blanket on the table and turned around to get something down from a high shelf. Tierza scrambled to the edge of the table by a chair, swung out over it, and hung by her hands for a second before she dropped onto the seat. Then she repeated the maneuver to get down to the floor. She landed on her rear with a hard bump and saw Rachel's feet turn around.

"Oh, Tierza," Rachel sighed, bending over to look under the table.

The little girl was already running. She darted from under the table and headed for the door. But it was closed and the gap underneath was too small for crawling through. As Rachel came around the table, Tierza changed her course and ran for the cabinets. There was a gap under those, and a piece of wood had broken away in one spot to open a hole into the three-inch high space.

She glanced back and saw Rachel just behind her, reaching down with a butterfly net to catch her. Tierza jumped for the hole and scrambled through on her hands and knees. A cloud of dust swarmed around her, but the particles were too big to make her sneeze.

Tierza bumped against a wall and turned around, curling up on her side facing the hole. Rachel's eye appeared in the opening.

"Clever little girl," the woman said, sounding frustrated. "I'll have to have this hole patched up someday."

As the adrenaline began to wear off, Tierza surprised herself by giggling. She'd gotten away from the giant woman. Sure, she was probably trapped in this dark, dusty hole, but she enjoyed the moment of victory.

Rachel groaned and stood up, and a moment later, Tierza heard the door open and close. But it didn't sound like it had shut all the way. She might be able to squeeze through.

She crawled closer to the opening and then stopped and listened. All she could hear was the hum of her little heart and the plip-plip sounds of dust settling around her.

Rachel must have left the room. Holding her breath, Tierza crawled farther and peered out. She saw no sign of the woman. A little farther...and a little more...

Soon she emerged completely from the hole and scrambled to her feet. She dashed to the end of the cabinets and peeped around the corner.

No Rachel, and the door was open a crack. Heedlessly she ran for it, and when she was just inches away, it swung open, nearly hitting her. She sprawled to the floor and the butterfly net slammed down inches from her.

With a terrified squeak Tierza jumped up and raced back to the cabinets, narrowly escaping the net a second time. She scurried into the dusty hole again and curled up.

Rachel glared in at her. She would have giggled again, but she wasn't enjoying this game anymore. The woman was getting angry, and that meant she would be more likely to hurt her.

Tierza began to cry. She wondered how much longer it would be until Jase's mom came to get her. She wanted to go home. Well, back to whatever home she had with Jase. It was the best she had in this giant, frightening world.

"All right, if that's how you want to play," Rachel said, getting up again. Tierza heard the door close just like last time, but she didn't move.

After a few minutes Rachel came back and looked through the hole. She pushed something large and shiny into view. "See this?" she said. "It's a hammer. And this is a nail." Then she slid something over the hole, and her muffled voice continued from the other side. "This is a block of wood. I decided to patch this hole myself so my patients can't hide under there."

There was an extremely loud bang that made Tierza jump and slam her head into the low roof. She scrambled to the hole and pushed against the block of wood, but it was immovable.

"No, please, let me out!" she screamed.

Her tiny voice was drowned out by the hammering. Every blow shook her whole body, and she cowered on the floor, holding her hands over her ears and whimpering.

After a minute the banging stopped, and Tierza slowly raised her throbbing head. She shoved the block of wood, but it was as immovable as before.

She began to panic and pounded on it with her fists. "Let me out!" she shrieked.

"Will you come nicely now?" Rachel asked. "Because if you run back in there, I'll close the hole up again and leave you there all day."

"I'll be good, I promise," Tierza cried, pressing herself against the wood and sobbing.

There was a thud and then the wood moved a bit. The two metal claws of the hammer worked their way through a gap and then the whole thing came free.

Tierza scrambled out and collapsed in a heap on the floor. The butterfly net scooped her up and she flopped awkwardly onto her back in the bottom of it, arms and legs flailing.

Rachel held her up. "I warned you," she said, shaking her head.

"I'll...I won't run anymore," Tierza sobbed.

"That's right." Rachel carried her across the room and opened one of the empty cages.

"No, please, not a cage!"

The fingers lifted her out of the net and dropped her into the cage, and then slammed the door shut. Tierza scrambled into the corner and curled up, shivering and crying.

Rachel's face loomed in front of her. "Well I'll be...she's acting just like a little *animal* caught in a cage. Tell me, Tierza, why do you feel threatened?"

The little girl didn't deign to answer her tormenter.

"I've always been curious about how and why animals have an innate fear of people. You seem to have that same fear, even of someone who's tried to be very gentle with you, and healed your broken ribs. Even of someone whose speech you can understand, which puzzles me. I always thought it would be easier if I could talk to an animal and assure it I meant no harm. But if you are any indication, maybe not—"

Tierza blocked out the voice by shoving her fingers in her ears. This overtly curious woman talked too much. She should try shutting up for once and paying attention to other people. Maybe then she would learn what she wanted to know.

Rachel left Tierza there and started getting out equipment. Tierza lost herself in her frightened thoughts and vague memories. In her mind she saw a heavy door slam shut over and over again, and it wasn't this one.

After a while Rachel came back, opened the cage, and took the little girl out. Tierza remained limp, resolved to let the woman do what she wanted.

But Rachel didn't trust her anymore, so the first thing that happened was getting strapped down to a board, her arms and legs spread out and immovable. She tried very hard not to panic, and only cried a little.

Rachel dabbed at the girl's tiny cheeks with a cotton swab. "You don't need to cry. I'm not going to hurt you."

It didn't make any difference to Tierza. She was powerless, and that was what terrified her. The fact was that the woman *could* hurt her, and she wouldn't be able to do anything about it.

Rachel wiped a funny smelling liquid on the girl's arm and then took a small, thin needle and poked it in. Tierza couldn't feel more than a dull sensation of something in her arm, but she had to close her eyes and clench her jaw to keep from shrieking.

When the needle came out she opened her eyes and saw that it had taken some of her blood. It was nice red blood, and she felt sick looking at it.

For another hour, Rachel Lindon examined Tierza, scanned her with various machines, measured her, and felt all over her tiny body.

At the end of that time, the little girl was glad to go back to her cage, curl her arms and legs that were sore from being kept straight too long, and cry herself to sleep.

Chapter Six

Running Again

Rayna parked outside Miss Lindon's animal clinic right at five-fifteen, as she had said. She went inside and nodded to the plump young lady behind the desk. "I'm here to see Rachel Lindon."

"She's in that room," the young woman said, pointing.

Rayna opened the door and found Miss Lindon standing over a table, talking in a low tone to Tierza. The little girl lay limp on the folded-blanket bed with her eyes closed.

"Ah, Rayna." Miss Lindon straightened up and met her in the doorway. "I'd like a word with you."

Rayna frowned and allowed the younger woman to step out of the room with her and close the door.

"Tierza might tell you some wild tales about today," Miss Lindon said. "The truth is, I had to restrain her for her own good. She's mostly healed, but she tried to run away, and I'm sure you'll agree that it would be an awful fate for her if she were to venture out and encounter a dog or a cat or—heaven forbid—a car."

Rayna nodded. "Yes, it would."

"I did a routine examination, and I'm afraid it bothered her. But it was nothing out of the ordinary, and I treated her as carefully as any of my most valuable charges."

Yes, Rayna thought, maybe so, but those were still animals. Was Tierza an animal?

She thought it, but she didn't say it. Instead she just nodded and said, "I'm sure you treated her well. Why are you telling me all this?"

Miss Lindon smiled. "I've never had a patient that could talk. Well, I've treated parrots, but they really just repeat everything. They couldn't relate a story of something that happened to them like Tierza can. I'm afraid she will give you an embellished horror story, and I want you to know the truth."

Rayna felt uncomfortable, but she nodded. "All right. Thanks."

They went back into the room and said goodbye and Rayna took Tierza out to the car, making sure she was completely covered during the transfer.

When they were moving, Tierza folded the top of the handkerchief down and looked up at Rayna.

"How was your day?" Rayna asked, feeling awkward. It didn't seem like the right thing to ask.

Tierza just stared at her.

"That bad?"

"She put me in a cage," Tierza muttered, lowering her gaze.

Rayna's heart clenched at the little girl's tone. So simple, yet it carried a tremendous weight of fear. "She did? Why?"

Tierza shuddered a little under her blanket and her tiny fingers appeared from beneath to grip the edge under her chin. "She locked me in a clear box and put it in a dark place, so I tried to run away."

"The x-ray machine? Oh, Tierza, she had to check your broken ribs."

"They aren't broken anymore."

"But she didn't know. Never mind. You ran away? How far did you get?"

"I couldn't get out of the room, so I crawled under a cabinet."

"How'd Rachel get you out?" Rayna glanced at the little girl and saw her go pale and shiver.

"She put something over the hole and locked me in until I panicked and screamed."

Something about Tierza's words made them sound absolutely true. Her voice was low and flat, speaking of terror as a thing of the past. No crying and whining. Just a simple statement of truth. This didn't sound like an embellished horror story. But Rayna had two kids; she knew how convincing they can be sometimes.

"Then what happened?" Rayna asked.

"She let me out and took out some of my blood and poked me and did other things."

A routine examination. Taking a small blood sample wasn't so out of the ordinary, was it?

"Don't make me go back," Tierza pleaded.

"You probably won't have to spend the day there again. If you're healed, you should be all right staying at home."

She wasn't sure that she wanted the little thing alone in her house all day, though. She could think of all sorts of things that could go wrong, for Tierza or for other things.

"Alone?"

Rayna nodded, noting just how shaken the miniature girl sounded.

"Can't Jase stay with me?"

The woman smiled. She'd always been fascinated by her son's gentle nature. He was certainly made for taking care of something vulnerable.

"Jase has school," she said. "But it's almost summer, and then he'll have a few months free."

After that Tierza went quiet and refused to answer any more questions, instead hiding behind her blanket and brooding.

When they got home, Jase was waiting at the door to take Tierza and rush her into his room.

"Are you healed yet?" he asked.

He set her on the desk, so she stood up and climbed off the folded blanket, stretching her arms above her head.

"I'm better," she said. "Still a little sore."

"I really wish you could come to school with me. Everyone would be so jealous that I have a friend who's twelve inches tall."

She shuddered and wrapped her arms around herself. "Not everyone is as nice as you."

He smiled, and then frowned. "You look pale. I mean, more pale than usual. Did something happen?"

She didn't feel like recounting her adventures again, so she just shrugged. "I'll be all right," she said.

Jase let the subject drop and they spent the next half hour until dinner was ready looking at the faerie book from the library.

Tierza tried to forget what happened, remembering that Rayna had said she wouldn't have to stay with Rotten Rachel Lindon again. But she couldn't get the cage out of her mind. It, and the x-ray machine, had awakened memories in the back of her mind that she didn't quite understand. Not that she wanted to. They weren't happy memories.

After dinner, which was mostly banana for Tierza, she was alone in Jase's room when she heard raised voices in the hallway outside the door. She climbed down from the desk to the chair, and then to the floor, and ran across the room. Standing by the doorway, she listened to the conversation, making sure she was out of the way if anyone suddenly pushed the door open.

"...don't raise your voice with me, Jase," Rayna said in a stern tone. "I run this house, and I have ever since your father left. You don't get to question my authority like that until you're a grownup yourself."

"Sorry Mom. But you just said Miss Lindon scared Tierza! Why would we send her back?"

Tierza stiffened, her heart racing.

"Miss Lindon is a trained veterinarian, and she was only looking out for the little creature's health."

"Creature? Isn't Tierza a person?"

"I don't know. I think we should find out what she is, like you want to. But when none of us are here, I don't really want her running loose in the house."

Jase grumbled something that Tierza couldn't hear, but she didn't care. She backed away from the door, wondering what Rayna really thought of her. Just an animal? Maybe that's what she was, a stupid animal that could talk.

She went across the room and crawled behind Jase's desk, where she could be surrounded by strong walls and at least feel safe for a bit.

Tierza cried for a moment and then stifled her tears. They were going to take her back to Miss Lindon in the morning, she just knew it. She would be an animal for a day, living in a cage and being experimented on.

Not if they couldn't find her, though. She wondered where would be the best place to hide. And then she wondered if she should even stay here. It wasn't where she belonged. Somewhere, she was sure, there were other small people like her. She just had to find them.

She heard Jase come back into the room, and she held her breath so he wouldn't hear her sobs.

"Tierza?" he called. "Where are you?"

She didn't answer. She stayed where she was for the

rest of the evening and didn't ever answer him. Jase looked all over for her, and then voiced his thoughts out loud that she could hide if she wanted to, as long as she didn't get herself stuck or hurt somewhere. He didn't manage to find her before bedtime.

Tierza waited until Jase was asleep, and then she crawled from behind the desk. Using a toy truck as a stepstool, she heaved an empty cardboard box onto the chair and climbed up after it. Using the box, she got up on the desk.

She knew exactly what she wanted. Grabbing the scissors, she climbed back down and then pulled the truck over to the bed. Standing tiptoe on it, she just managed to get her hands over the edge and pulled herself up beside the large lump that was Jase.

Careful not to touch the boy too much, she stepped over his ankles and made her way across the wrinkled blanket to the windowsill. Jase rolled over just after she got past, a move that would have trapped her in the blanket and maybe squashed her if she'd been just a little slower.

The window was open a couple inches, and covered with a screen. She'd figured that out by paying attention, and she was proud of herself for thinking of it. She pressed the points of the scissors against the screen and leaned all her weight into it. It took a lot of effort, but finally the blades went through, cutting an inch-wide slit.

Tierza pulled the scissors out of the slit and used them to widen it to about three inches. Then she set them aside and looked back at Jase.

"Thanks," she whispered. "For being nice to me."

Then she wriggled through the screen, dangled from the slit for a moment, and dropped to the ground. She smacked against the side of the house when her feet hit, and then sprawled backward in the grass.

Tierza sat up and shivered, then climbed unsteadily to her feet. A sudden pain stabbed her chest and she leaned against the wall and breathed carefully until it went away.

She stared out into the night with wide eyes, afraid of going forward and afraid of going back. The world behind wasn't where she belonged, and made her feel powerless about what happened to her. The world before her was large, dark, and cold, but somewhere out there was the place she belonged.

Chapter Seven

The Window Beast

On unsteady legs Tierza started to walk away from the house. She'd hardly gone five steps when a large shape rounded the corner. She yelped and laid down flat, hoping the grass would hide her.

As she raised her head slowly to get a look, she saw a face she recognized and dreaded. The thing that had looked in the window. She knew it was a boy like Jase, though he was probably nothing like Jase at all. His face wasn't glowing this time, but he held the source of the light in his hand.

He was heading for the window again, and Tierza realized he'd be standing almost on top of her. She scrambled away, but it was too much movement. The

boy loomed over her, keeping her in a circle of light from his hand. She gave up crawling and got to her feet to run, but fingers wrapped around her chest and lifted her clear off the ground. She started to scream, but something hit her head and knocked her mostly senseless.

Tierza thought she heard a door closing, but the next thing she knew for sure was a blazing flood of light in her face. She scrunched her eyes shut and put her hands to the sides of her head, trying to squeeze out the headache.

After a moment, she became aware that she was lying flat on her back on something hard. Her eyes adjusted to the light and she saw that hideous face staring down at her with a grin.

Tierza sat up, wobbling a bit, and coughed. The boy cupped his hands around her so she couldn't run, and her shoulders slumped in resignation.

"So, what is this?" the boy muttered.

"What do you want?" Tierza whimpered. "Please let me go!"

The boy's eyes got wide and he poked her with a fingertip, setting off a crushing pain in her chest. She would have protested, or cried, or screamed, but she was too busy trying to breathe.

"Do you have a name?" he asked.

"Why would I tell you?"

He thumped her on the head and her headache got worse. "Because you're little and I'm big," he said.

"Tierza Velvet," she muttered. "But Jase named me."

"Jase." The boy said the name with scorn. "Jase is a weenie."

"He didn't hurt me."

The boy poked her again and this time the pain was so much that she collapsed back on the desk. "That's 'cause he's a weenie. I'm not a weenie. I'm Philip, but you can call me Master."

"No."

He flicked her in the side and she arched her back and screamed. Quickly he pressed a giant finger over her mouth to stifle her. He smashed her upper lip into her teeth so hard it began to bleed.

"Be quiet," Philip ordered. "I'm supposed to be in bed. You know what would happen if my Mom found you? Whoosh! Down the toilet."

Tierza shuddered and bit his finger. He jerked it away, but she shut her mouth and sobbed quietly, licking blood from the inside of her lips.

"No biting," he snapped.

"You're hurting me!" she cried. Her chest ached almost as much as it had right after Miss Lindon bandaged it.

"I'm big, so I'm the one in charge here. Stand up."

Tierza rolled over and struggled to get up on her knees. Every little movement sent stabbing bursts of pain through her chest.

"You move so slow," Philip griped.

She collapsed, and let out an anguished cry as her chest hit the desk. She should've stayed with Jase. Even Miss Lindon was better than this. But no, she had to be dumb and try to run away. Would Jase be able to find her? Or would she be tormented here until Philip's mother found her and did something terrible? Well, maybe she would deserve it for thinking she could do things on her own.

"That wasn't standing up," the boy said. He grabbed her by one shoulder and lifted her up, holding so tightly that he gave her some huge, deep bruises.

When he let go she swayed on her shaky legs, but managed to stay upright. She gritted her teeth and tried not to scream.

"Better. Now, can you fly? Do you have wings?"

"No! But I have broken ribs and you made them worse."

He made a disgusted face. "Don't blame it all on me."

She shut her eyes tightly and tiny tears squeezed out of them.

"You know what?" Philip said. "You aren't the first tiny person I've seen."

Tierza opened her eyes and stared at him. Really? Could he know something that would help her find where she belonged? Assuming she got away from him alive.

"Why are you so surprised? Logically, there should be more people like you, 'cause you must have had parents."

"Where?" she asked.

"Huh?"

"Where was the other little person you saw?"

"In San Francisco. It was near the Golden Gate Bridge. The little person there had wings, and I saw it fly up into the sky and disappear."

Your flight is forfeit, young one. You are no longer one of us.

Tierza blinked and shook her head at the voice that had jumped out of her blank past.

"At the time I thought I was crazy," Philip said. "And I did until I saw you on the shelf while I was spying on Jase."

She shuddered, thinking of this cruel boy watching her sleep and likely plotting to steal her. And then she'd walked right into his hands.

He leaned on the desk and peered at her. "I wonder if you're a real person or some sort of animal."

Tierza sank to her knees, sweaty and dizzy. She didn't really know, and maybe she didn't care. It was just a title, that was all. If she was an animal, she could still talk and think.

There was a single knock on the door and Philip jumped.

"You should be in bed trying to sleep," a woman's voice warned. "Not having conversations with yourself with the light on."

Philip rolled his eyes and grabbed Tierza. "We'll talk in the morning," he hissed. "And I'll take you to school to show all my friends. They'll be so jealous."

Then he dropped her into a cardboard box, closed up the top, and slid it under his bed. She crawled into the corner of the box and curled up on her side, the one that didn't have hurt ribs. She wondered if the ribs were broken again, and if she would ever heal.

Tierza took a deep breath and stifled her sobs. Nobody was going to find her here, and shedding tears wouldn't make anything better. It would be best to get some sleep, and hope to be rescued before Philip killed her.

Being injured and exhausted, it didn't take long for her to fall asleep, despite her fear.

When Jase got up in the morning, and the first thing he did was check Tierza's bed. It wasn't arranged any differently than the night before. The little girl hadn't slept in it.

"Mom!"

He found her in the kitchen, assembling three sack lunches, for him, Nikka, and herself.

"What do you want, Jason? Don't forget to brush your teeth before you leave for school."

"Mom, Tierza's gone! She didn't sleep in her bed last night."

"Are you sure?"

"Yes. She's just gone!"

"Could she have gotten out of your room?"

Jase shrugged. "Probably, but where would she go?"

"I don't know. Check your window, she might have gotten out that way."

Muttering under his breath, Jase went back to his room and flopped over his bed to look at the window. He froze and blinked, and then felt the split in the screen. With a sinking heart he picked up the scissors that lay on the sill and went back to the kitchen.

"Yeah, she got out the window." He sighed. "She used these to cut the screen."

"I'm sorry," Rayna said, folding over the top of a paper bag and handing it to him. "There's your lunch. Maybe Tierza decided she didn't want to stay here."

"You don't care, do you?" Tears stung Jase's eyes. "How could she take care of herself out there? She's so...tiny."

"Jason, of course I care. But if she decided to leave, there's not much we can do about that, is there?"

"She'll get killed," he muttered. "I can't believe she would just leave like that." Then he looked up at Rayna. "Maybe it's because of Miss Lindon."

"Did you tell Tierza she had to go back there today?"

"No! I couldn't find her. But she could've overheard us talking."

Rayna patted his shoulder. "We can just hope that she'll come back if she needs help. Now stop worrying and get ready for school."

Jase didn't stop worrying. He got ready with a heavy heart and then stepped outside into the bright, late-spring sunlight. The bus wasn't there yet, so he wandered out into the yard and kicked at the uneven tufts of grass as he waited. If his father was there...

No, he shouldn't think that. Things were how they were for a reason.

"Hey, Juice!"

Jase groaned and looked at the bully who just happened to live a few blocks away. Philip climbed over the fence into the yard with a grin.

"You look upset," the bully observed. "Something wrong?"

"No," Jase muttered.

"I don't believe you. But anyway, I have something cool to show all the guys at school."

"What?"

"It's a secret. I don't even think I'll show you. I just wanted to tell you so you can burn with curiosity."

"I don't care what you have," Jase said with a yawn.

"Sure you do. You're dying to know, especially since I won't tell you now."

"I said I don't care! Leave me alone."

Philip stayed right where he was. "Did you lose something?"

Jase eyed him suspiciously. "Why do you ask?"

The other boy shrugged with a slight smirk. "It seemed like you were looking for something."

"I was just wandering around and kicking the grass for no reason. Now leave me alone."

At that moment the bus pulled up, so they were spared any further conversation. Jase sat way up in the front, because he knew Philip would never be seen there, the domain of the nerds and the friendless. Cool kids sat in the back. The dumb ones who tried to make up for their lack of neurons by acting cool.

All the way to school, Jase couldn't get his mind off Philip's comments. What if the bully had found Tierza? The thought was almost enough to make him cry. But crying in public was a bad idea, so he kept it all in and it made him feel sick.

Chapter Eight

It Comes To Blows

Tierza could hear Philip and Jase talking, but she was wrapped up in a towel and shoved into the backpack, stuffed in so tightly she nearly suffocated. Whatever feeble screams she managed to get out were muffled by the fabric.

Every time Philip moved, his books shifted and jolted her, setting off sharp pains in her chest. Soon she had to focus all her strength on breathing just to stay alive. Tiny tears dripped down her cheeks to moisten the towel that covered her face. A few times she got so exhausted she almost gave up struggling, but a moment later she'd come to life again, fighting for air.

After a while, she heard the noise of a big crowd, and Philip was walking again. She started seeing flashes of phantom light, but tried to stay conscious. If she passed out she might miss a chance to escape.

There was a metallic clang and then she heard Philip's voice.

"Hey, guys, I've got something to show you."

The backpack gave a sickening lurch and she gasped.

"Now, you have to promise to keep this a secret. All right?"

There were a few expressions of agreement. Then the zipper screeched and light flooded in. Philip took her out and unwrapped the towel until she lay limp over his hand, staring at the floor. Her head ached and she felt like she was going to throw up.

Philip and a few other boys were huddled against a wall of lockers to block her from the sight of anyone else who happened by. When Philip turned her over in his hands, she saw through half-opened eyelids the speechless shock on the faces of three other boys.

"What is that?" one of them asked.

"I don't know. She said her name's Tierza Velvet."

"Dude, it can talk?" another blurted.

"Yeah."

"Make it talk," the first boy said.

Philip poked her in the belly and she tensed with a gasp. "C'mon, Tierza, say something."

She just moaned and closed her eyes.

"Hey, can I hold it?"

"Not now. Maybe later."

Then Tierza heard Jase's voice, and her heart leapt. She peeked with one eye to see him shove between two of the boys, who were all bigger than him, and grab Philip by the shoulder.

"You did steal her!" Jase cried, and she saw tears in his eyes.

"You calling me a thief?"

"A thief and a bully. Tierza is just a little person, and you're hurting her!"

"And what are you going to do about it?"

"This..." Jase swung a fist and punched Philip square in the left eyeball. At the same time he grabbed for Tierza with his other hand. His fingers closed around her just as the other boys grabbed him from behind and jerked him back.

"Aagh! You little thug!" Philip held one hand over his hurt eye and glared with the other at Jase. And at the little girl in his hand.

Jase suddenly stooped and set her on the floor. "Run!" he hissed.

Philip grabbed for her, but a surge of adrenaline kicked in and she lurched between Jase's feet and ran down the hall, keeping near the wall to avoid the crushing feet all around.

Jase cried out in pain behind her, and she clenched her jaw and kept running. People who caught sight of her gave exclamations of surprise and alarm. Someone was chasing her, but they had to push through the flood of huge people and quickly fell behind. Crying and gasping for air, she reached the entrance of the building, where the doors were propped open, and darted outside.

To escape the flood of humans she left the walkway, running through knee-high grass until she came to some small shrubs. Into one of these she crawled and sat with her back against the trunk.

Then the adrenaline faded and she began shaking. The pain in her chest came back worse than before, and she sagged against the rough wood, watching all the big people moving around on the walkway. Nobody could see her in here, but since she could see them, it still seemed like they'd see her if they looked.

Tierza hugged herself and swallowed her sobs, thinking of what was happening to Jase. He wasn't as small as her, but he was smaller than those other boys. And outnumbered. And it was her fault.

She had to leave now, so people wouldn't have to fight over her. She would try to get to San Francisco and find more little people like her.

But wait. Jase was getting hurt because she ran away.

What should she do?

Tierza curled up in the dirt, beginning to breathe easier. No matter what, she couldn't help Jase. She was just a tiny little girl that everyone wanted to touch and hold. And Jase tried so hard to help her, but he couldn't really. The most he'd done so far was take her place as the object of Philip's cruelty. If she left, he wouldn't have to try to protect her anymore, and maybe he wouldn't get hurt.

She sat up and took as deep a breath as she could. Then she stood, leaning against the shrub's trunk for support. Her legs shook, and the pain in her chest made her dizzy. But she stumbled out of the shrub and limped across the huge lawn, away from all the people. Always away from the people.

Jase had swollen, bloody lips, a bleeding nose, and plenty of ugly bruises. Philip sat across from him in the hallway outside the principle's office, filling the air between them with a murderous scowl. The bigger boy had suffered that first solid punch, but no more, so he only had a single black eye. It made him look even more menacing.

Consequences would be serious, and Jase hardly thought about the physical pain. This wasn't the first time he and Philip had fought, though it was definitely the worst. He briefly wondered if either of them would be expelled. Probably not. But they'd be suspended at least. Jase's mom would be upset, to put it mildly, and Philip would be looking for revenge.

At least Tierza got away. But where had she gone? He told her to run, and she did, but he had no idea if she was safe or if someone else had caught her and shoved her into their own backpack.

Finally Philip's mother arrived. She frowned at her son, but gave Jase an even darker scowl. After a short time in the principle's office, she came out and left with Philip.

A few minutes later Jase's mom showed up. She too was frowning, but she actually talked to him.

"What happened this time, Jason?"

"Philip had Tierza!" he said. "He was hurting her, so I attacked him and his friends so she could get away."

Rayna sighed, but he could see a faint spark of admiration in her eyes. She ruffled his hair and went into the office.

For a few minutes Jase fidgeted in his seat, wondering what would happen when they got home. He'd just seen something in his mom that he hadn't seen before.

When she came back out, she gave him a tiny smile and they walked out to the car together. He watched for Tierza, especially when they got outside, hoping that she would see them and they could take her home. Rayna seemed to be doing the same thing, but when they reached the car there was no sign of the little girl.

Jase kept his mouth shut, knowing that starting a conversation could mean disaster. So the drive home was quiet, until they parked outside the house.

Then his mother turned to him. "Jase, you should know that I'm proud of you for standing up for Tierza. But you started a fight, and that's not something I want you to do. Ever."

"I didn't start it, Mom. Philip did when he hurt Tierza." Jase climbed out of the car, listening for an answer.

In fact, Rayna didn't have a rebuttal to that. She seemed to be inclined to agree with him. "Just be wise," she said when they entered the house. "There will be times when you have to fight, but there's usually a better choice."

Tierza didn't know where she was. She had no idea how to get to San Francisco, nor did she know how far away it was. The street she followed away from the school entered a neighborhood, and she ran from bush to tree to bush, always dreading that a dog or cat would be running loose and chase her. She saw a few dogs, but they were all behind fences.

She must have been walking for hours when she heard her name called. For a long time she'd moved in short bursts, resting for a few minutes at each hiding place. She was dirty, exhausted, and tired of being in such pain that she could barely breathe.

So when she heard Nikka's voice shouting her name, she wasn't surprised at the sudden hope that filled her heart. Tierza wanted to go back with them, even if they had Miss Lindon take care of her during the day. At least with them she had a safe place to sleep.

Tierza crawled out of the bush she was hiding in and ran out toward the road. Nikka was driving along in her car with her head out the window, shouting Tierza's name every few yards.

Ferocious barking made the little girl turn around, and from farther up the street she saw a bulldog streaking toward her.

With a terrified yelp she pushed herself faster. Nikka saw her and drove the car into the curb, jumping out before it even stopped moving.

Tierza collapsed at Nikka's feet just as the bulldog caught up with her.

Chapter Nine

Nikka's Room

Nikka snatched up the little girl and kicked the bulldog in the face. It bounced back and whimpered, looking much smaller from this new perspective, Tierza thought. She flopped over Nikka's hand with a strangled sob as the dog retreated.

In the car, she realized that her rescuer was shaking. Nikka set her on the passenger seat, closed the driver's door, and leaned on the steering wheel.

"Are you all right?" Nikka asked after a moment.

"Yes...what's wrong with you?"

Nikka started the car and gave a small, nervous laugh. "Oh, I couldn't help imagining what would have happened if I was just a few seconds later. Sorry."

Tierza shivered. What would have happened? She would have died in the jaws of that dog, most likely. "Thank you," she said.

"No problem. Just don't run off again."

"I won't. I promise."

"Good. Mom has a promise to make too, regarding Rachel Lindon."

Tierza lay down flat on the seat to rest her aching body. Exhaustion caught up with her and she blinked a few times before allowing her eyes to close.

The slam of the car door startled Tierza out of sleep and she started to sit up, only to flop back down at a sharp stab of pain. Nikka opened the passenger door and gently picked her up.

"Just relax, Tierza."

She did. They went inside, where Rayna was making dinner and Jase sat at the table hunched over some books.

"I found her," Nikka said.

Jase leapt up from the table and rushed across the room. "Tierza!" he cried. "Are you okay?"

She shifted a little, and winced as the pain flared up again. It wasn't so bad now; either she'd been running so long that she was numb to it, or her body was healing.

"I'll be all right," she said.

Nikka set her on the table and sat down opposite from Jase's place. He took his seat again, and Tierza sat up, leaning back on her hands.

"We need to decide what we're going to do now," Nikka said. "Mom?"

"Just a minute."

"San Francisco!" Jase said. "That's where the box came from, so that's where she came from."

Rayna came and joined them at the table. "We can't just run off to San Francisco. I have work, and you two have school. It's almost four hours one way."

"The weekend, Mom," Jase said. "We could go there on Saturday, spend the night, and come back on Sunday evening. Then we would have almost two days to look around."

"And what would we look for?"

Tierza tried to sit up straighter. "Um..." she said.

They all looked at her.

"That mean boy—Philip—he said he saw another tiny person in San Francisco." She didn't mention that it had wings. Would they believe her if she did?

"I don't trust Philip," Jase grumbled.

"He wasn't so surprised to see me," Tierza said. "I think it was the truth."

"Supposing it is," Rayna said, "did he mention where he saw this tiny person?"

"I think...he said by the Golden Gate Bridge." She wrinkled her nose in a frown. "What's that?"

"Only the most awesome bridge in the world," Jase said with a wide grin. "I wish I could live on top of one of the towers."

"In the wind and rain?" Nikka asked.

"No, silly, I'd have them build a little house up there. And I'd have a roller coaster that goes up and down the cables."

"We're talking about Tierza right now," Rayna said.

Jase nodded. "Can we go to San Francisco this weekend? Please, Mom?"

"You don't need to beg. I think we can manage that."

"Can we visit Dad on the way?" Nikka asked.

Tierza was puzzled at Rayna's reaction. The woman suddenly looked older and very tired. And all she said was 'maybe.'

"I can't wait to see the bridge again," Jase said, leaning forward and speaking to the little girl as if he hadn't noticed his mother's mood. "You'll love it, I'm sure. It's so huge and red and amazing."

Rayna stood up. "Until Saturday, Tierza, you can stay in Nikka's room. You don't have to go back to Miss Lindon."

"Why not my room?" Jase asked.

"Nikka is upstairs. It'll be...safer."

Tierza figured Rayna was worried about her running away again. But she liked the idea. Philip wouldn't be able to look in through the window at night. At least, she hoped he wouldn't.

"Is that all right?"

The little girl blinked. "Huh? Oh, yes, I think so. Thank you."

Nikka chuckled.

"That's it then," Rayna said. "Get your homework done, kids."

Rayna went back to the kitchen, and Nikka scooped up Tierza and carried her up the stairs to a new room she hadn't seen before.

It was nothing like Jase's. The boy had posters and pictures all over his walls, a perpetually messy bed, and lots of junk. Nikka had just one huge picture of a city on her wall, organized shelves, and a smooth colorful quilt over the bed. Even her little desk was tidy, with books and papers in stacks, pencils and pens all sticking out of a mug like the branches of a spiky bush.

Nikka set her on the fluffy pillow and then pulled a chair from the corner and sat down facing the bed.

"You like it?"

Tierza stopped gazing around at all the colors and smiled. "It's nice."

"I wanted the walls dark purple, but Mom thought it would be too depressing, so when we remodeled we went with lavender."

"Oh." Tierza wasn't quite sure what that all meant, but she liked the color of the walls.

Nikka leaned forward, resting her elbows on her knees and her chin in her hands. "So," she said. "Have you remembered anything at all?"

The little girl felt the blood drain from her face as she remembered her last flashback. *Your flight is forfeit, young one. You are no longer one of us.*

What did it mean? Philip said the person he saw by the bridge had wings.

Did she used to have wings?

"Tierza? Are you all right?"

She blinked and suddenly felt dizzy. Next thing she knew, she was lying on her side. Nikka moved quickly to the bed and lifted the little girl in gentle hands.

"Something's wrong. What's wrong?"

Nikka's voice sounded almost frantic, and Tierza wondered if she really looked that bad. What was wrong anyway? She was weak and injured, plagued by disturbing memories that she couldn't quite remember. How would that make her collapse?

"I'm exhausted," she whispered.

"Oh! Have you eaten at all today? You've been running around all day..."

"No."

Nikka stood up. "You wait here and I'll go get you a piece of banana." She laid the little girl back on the pillow and rushed out of the room.

Tierza was more concerned with her mind than her stomach. Wings? The idea of having had them at some point seemed bizarre. Tierza reached around and felt her back, pushing her hand up under her shirt. Her skin was smooth, not even scarred. As far as she could tell from feeling it. She would have to check in the mirror.

No, that was silly. She didn't have wings now, so why would she have ever had them? How would they have been removed?

She sighed. It would make more sense if she never had wings. Maybe all the other little people like her had wings, and she was born without them, so they rejected her.

But what could her flashback mean then? How could she forfeit something she never had? Assuming the voice was talking to her. She must have had some way of flying. So she must have had wings at one point.

Tears pricked her eyes and she turned onto her side to curl up. She was confused now, and it made her more afraid.

After a minute, Nikka returned and stooped over her.

"Tierza? Are you crying?"

The little girl scrubbed her eyes and shook her head. She sat up and took a small piece of banana, avoiding Nikka's gaze as she ate.

"You *were* crying. What's wrong? Don't you feel safe here?"

"Yes. But...I don't belong here. That's why I ran away. I'm like a pet to you."

"No, of course not! At least, not to me. I think you're a real person, no matter how small you are. And I'm sure Jase thinks the same."

"Not Miss Lindon. She locked me up and poked me." Tierza shuddered. "And I couldn't do anything about it!"

Nikka looked glum. "I know. I heard about that. But I don't think she realized how it upset you. No. Don't worry about that. Rachel Lindon won't bother you anymore."

The little girl sniffed and frowned. "Okay..."

Nikka paced the room a couple times, and then she sat down and gave Tierza a sad smile. "Hey, you don't need to feel like you don't belong. We're not going to turn you out of the house."

Tierza's vision flashed white and a terrible pain sliced through her head.

"Tierza? Oh no. I think you really need help—"

"No!" the little girl cried in her stupor. "I didn't do it! Please, stop…"

Fingers closed around her and she jerked her head forward with a gasp. "No…Nikka?"

"What happened?"

Tierza turned cold and realized her shirt was soaked with sweat. How much time had passed? It had felt like only a few seconds.

"You're really pale," Nikka said. "I think someone should check you out."

"No! I'm fine now." Tierza paused to catch her breath. "It was…I remembered something."

Nikka's eyes were wide and wet. "What?" she asked.

"I…don't know for sure."

"I'm taking you to Mom. You might have a fever, but I don't know, you were already hot before."

Tierza curled up in the giant hands cupped around her and moaned as Nikka carried her downstairs. The flashback had gone but it left behind a bad headache.

If you cannot do it, you can pass the responsibility to me.

No...I'll do it.

You seem to hesitate, and I understand that. But this has to be done, Josiah. The ruling has been passed. You cannot save her from her fate.

I know. I know. If she must die like this, I want to have her life on my hands and on none other's.

You are afraid you will want revenge? I can understand. Here is the needle. Do it quickly while I watch.

She's so young...

You are stalling.

There, I did it. See? But I'll never forget. She is beautiful, Hector. I wish she could have had a full life first.

There is much pain ahead for this one. I am sorry, Josiah, I truly am. Be glad the ruling spared her from a worse fate. This is a merciful end, rather than some of the other punishments that could have been chosen.

But there is no chance for pardon.

No, there is not. The deed is done.

Chapter Ten

Road Trip

Rayna gave Tierza a tiny bit of crushed white pills mixed with water. They used an eyedropper to feed it to her, and Jase remarked that it was like feeding a baby bird. Nikka glared at him for that and he apologized.

Tierza hardly paid them any attention. Her head pounded, her throat hurt, and all her insides were on fire even though she felt like she was freezing. Jase brought her a soft cloth and they covered her with many layers of it. Still she felt cold.

"I think we'd better call a doctor," Rayna said.

Tierza shook her head.

"She said no, Mom," Jase said. "Let's just watch for a little while. If she gets worse we can call someone."

But Tierza didn't get worse. She warmed up, and Nikka said she was cooling down, and the headache faded away. After a couple hours, when Jase was getting ready for bed, she felt almost well again.

Nikka hadn't been away from her for more than a couple minutes all evening, and the little girl was glad for such a gentle friend. Jase wasn't bad at all, but Nikka seemed to understand her better.

After Jase went to bed, the girls went upstairs, and Nikka arranged the tiny bed on her nightstand, at the base of a towering blue lava lamp. Tierza lay there alone for a few minutes while the big girl brushed her teeth. And then Nikka turned off the ceiling lights, left the lava lamp on, and lay down on her side facing Tierza.

The room was almost silent. It wasn't a hard silence that made her want to hear something to break it, but a soft silence, like a winter night in the country when it's snowing big, fluffy flakes and there's already six inches of snow on the ground, and nearby is a little cabin with light spilling out its windows and smoke drifting from the chimney...

Tierza wondered where she got that image. It must have been something she'd once seen, but she couldn't remember it for sure. With a sigh she snuggled deeper into her bed and tried to forget that she couldn't remember her life. She was warm and safe now, and she wanted to be happy also.

"What's it like, being so small?" Nikka asked in a soft, murmuring voice.

Tierza thought for a moment. "I've never been big, I don't think. So how would I describe it?"

"Are you always scared?"

"No...I'm not scared now."

Nikka smiled. "Good. I really do hope you can stay. Of course, if you have a family and a home somewhere else, that's great. But if you don't..."

Tierza thought about her recurring flashbacks. They were so cryptic, but there was one thing she was almost certain of. Wherever she came from, the people there didn't want her back.

If she could only remember it all, maybe she could settle down here and leave the past alone. But she had to know who she was.

And the only way she would learn that, unless she remembered, would be to find someone who knew her.

Tierza rolled onto her side and curled up, watching the unearthly blue light from the lamp flow over Nikka's face in random patterns. Her eyelids grew heavy and she yawned, and the last thing she saw before she slept was Nikka's smile.

The next afternoon, Nikka insisted on washing Tierza's clothes, which were smudged with dirt and grass stains.

"But I don't have any others to wear," the little girl protested. "They'll be fine."

Nikka leaned down and sniffed. "You don't smell good, and clean clothes will feel so much better. I'll find something for you to wear. Now off with them."

Tierza gave in, and even let Nikka talk her into a bath in the sink. She came out trembling and freezing cold, and decided that she didn't like being wet. Nikka wrapped a washcloth around her and she wore that until her clothes were clean and dry.

They did feel a lot better when they were clean. Softer. And they smelled like flowers. Jase even commented on it at dinner that evening, and Nikka made a funny comment about boys never noticing stuff like that.

Tierza began to feel more like a person among them, less like an unusual little creature. Maybe it was just the novelty of her size wearing off, but however it happened, they were treating her like a nice little sister.

She liked that.

Saturday morning dawned as bright and clear as ever. The California summer had already begun, and the weatherman promised high temperatures with no clouds.

The week had been mostly uneventful. Tierza had a minor fever on Thursday afternoon, but it went away like before, and she asked them not to call any doctors.

Her flashbacks had ceased as well, though she wasn't sure if that was a good thing or a bad thing. It could mean that she wasn't going to remember any more of her life, or maybe it was just because she was healing, and eventually all her memories would reappear as if they'd never been gone.

But there was one strange thing that kept happening. Whenever Tierza got hungry, her heart would start beating irregularly and her breath would come hard. She didn't tell anyone about this, but it was so regular that it started to worry her. And it was getting worse, unless that was just the anxiety distorting her perception.

If it got too bad, she wouldn't want to hide it, even if she could. But until then, she didn't want them worrying about her and talking about doctors.

On Saturday morning, Nikka packed a backpack with a change of clothes and a few other items. Then they went downstairs and Nikka set Tierza on the counter and dropped her bag beside a small suitcase on the floor.

Rayna was making sandwiches, and Nikka made sure there were bananas in the cooler. Jase came out of his room lugging a bulging backpack that looked more than half his size.

"What do you have in there?" Nikka asked.

"Uh, just a lot of stuff. I couldn't decide what to bring, so I took it all."

"Good thing we have a big trunk."

Tierza peered over the rim of the cooler, standing on tiptoe to see into it. She jerked back when Rayna dropped a sandwich in, all wrapped in its clear plastic bag.

"You know what?" Jase said. "It's been a week since we found Tierza."

"People don't usually celebrate one-week anniversaries," Nikka said.

"Come on, could we at least go to Mike's place on the way?"

Rayna chuckled. "You just want an excuse to get ice cream."

"Hey, it's supposed to be hot today. Ice cream would be good."

"That's a good enough reason for me."

They left the house at about ten a.m. with three bags, a cooler, and a very agitated twelve-inch girl.

Tierza was afraid of what she might learn. She wanted to know about her past, but she was settling down with her new family, and part of her wished she could just stay and forget. The conflicting emotions tore her up inside, and she kept very quiet.

What if they found nothing, and returned home with no new knowledge about her? Maybe then she could lay her forgotten past to rest and live her new life.

They drove for a few minutes and then parked outside an ice cream shop.

"Oh...can we take Tierza in?" Jase asked.

"Not a good idea," Nikka said. "Let other people see her and we'll have news reporters all over us in no time."

"I'll stay here," Tierza offered.

Nikka settled back into her seat. "Me too. Bring me what I usually get."

"One gross minty ice cream sandwich," Jase said as he climbed out. "Of course."

Tierza climbed up on the armrest of Jase's door and peered out the window as Rayna and the boy went into the shop. Then she stepped down onto the seat and turned around.

Nikka smiled at her. "Are you excited?"

Tierza nodded. "And a little scared."

"Why? Is it just because we're going to new places?"

"No...I think...I'm afraid of what we might find out." Her throat tightened and she rubbed her eyes. "I like living with you. If I find out I have a real home, I'll have to choose."

"Aw, don't worry about that. Just enjoy the trip and worry about where you'll live when the time comes. You know, chances are we won't find out anything."

"You think so?" Tierza was surprised at how relieved she sounded. But shouldn't she be? She didn't want change, because change was uncomfortable.

"You really don't want to leave, do you?"

The little girl paused for a moment, and then shook her head as if she'd just decided it now. And maybe she had. "I have something to tell you," she began in an even smaller voice than before.

"About what?"

"Things I remembered." Tierza sat down and stretched her legs out in front of her, tapping her little sneakers together over and over again. "I had some flashbacks."

"I figured. What were they about?"

"Bad things." She shuddered. "Dark cells, and locked doors. Pain, lots of pain. And falling. And I remember a voice."

Nikka twisted around in the seat so she was sitting sideways and didn't have to turn her head so far. "A voice?"

"It says something like, 'Your flight is forfeit. You aren't one of us anymore.' It scares me. I think it's talking to me."

Nikka nodded slowly, her eyes wide. "Do you think you used to have wings? Might sound crazy, but then, so does a person twelve inches tall."

"I don't know! I felt my back and there aren't any scars. And you saw it when I had a bath. You didn't see any scars, did you? How would they take off my wings without leaving a mark? If I even had them to begin with."

"Well, if you did have wings, would that make you a faerie? And aren't faeries magical? Maybe they took them away magically."

Tierza's spine tingled. She didn't like that idea. "Philip said he saw a tiny person like me in San Francisco."

"Yes, you mentioned that."

"He said...he said the other little person had wings, and it flew into the sky."

"Really?"

"He said he thought he was crazy until he saw me."

"Wow. I thought the faerie idea was just something wild to chuckle about. Maybe it's more likely than I thought."

Tierza scooted over as Jase opened the door and climbed in. He had a plastic bowl of something in one hand, and a smaller cup in the other.

"Banana flavored ice cream!" he announced, handing her a tiny paper cup with a two-inch plastic spoon in it. "That's a sample. Perfect size for you."

Rayna slid into the driver's seat and they resumed the trip. Tierza licked ice cream off her spoon and shivered.

"It's so cold!" she said.

Jase chuckled. "Of course. That's why you eat it in the summer."

She licked some more and the sweet, creamy taste filled her mouth and flowed down her throat. It was like bananas from heaven, and she giggled. She pressed her anxiety into a far corner of her mind and listened to Jase telling insane stories about werewolves at school and teacher-eating plants for biology projects. The road trip was off to a good start.

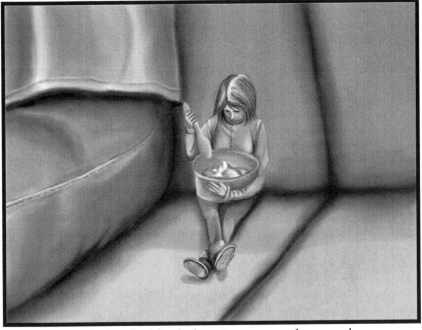

Until the flashback hit. It was maybe two hours later, and the ice cream was long gone, leaving sticky chins and fingers in the backseat. Tierza felt a sickening heat wash over her and she doubled over on the seat with a groan as everything else faded away.

You shouldn't have come back here. Don't you know what will happen if they find you?

Father, I...please, can't you do anything?

I tried. Believe me, I tried everything I could. Already I'm defying the Court by not killing you on sight.

Father! I didn't do it!

I believe you. But nobody else does. I can't do any more or they would condemn me too.

You wouldn't even run away with me?

I have your brothers and sisters and mother to look after. Should I take them all along to a similar fate? Look at me, Jera. I cried. I still cry. I hate this, but I'm trapped. You need to just go.

"I didn't do it!" she screamed. "I didn't do it!"

"Tierza, are you all right?"

The urgency of the voice broke through the haze and she blinked her eyes open. Jase cradled her in his hands, and Nikka looked back from the front seat with a worried expression. Rayna still drove, but she was asking if she should pull over.

"I didn't...do it." Tierza sobbed and rubbed her eyes. "I'm fine. Just...I don't know."

"What happened?" Nikka asked.

"I remembered something. My name."

Jase's eyes grew wider. "What is it?"

"Jera. I have a father somewhere. And a mother. And brothers and sisters."

Chapter Eleven

Golden Bridge

"Jera," Jase said. "It seems weird to call you that. You've always looked like Tierza to me."

"Keep calling me Tierza," she murmured. "I think Jera is supposed to be dead."

"Really?" Nikka asked, her eyes wide. "Do you remember any more?"

Tierza was remembering, and she didn't like it. She just nodded and bit her lip.

"If you remember, why don't you tell us?"

"Um...I think...they think I did something bad that I didn't do, and they sent me away."

"Then you can't go back," Jase said. "You could live with us!"

"Don't start assuming things ahead of what we know," Rayna said. "Let's first try to find out where she's from."

"Sure, Mom."

Tierza shivered and curled up in the boy's hands. Her stomach didn't feel very good.

"Uh oh," Jase said. "Are you still sick?"

She moaned and swallowed hard. She was going to throw up. "I'm not...feeling..."

Tierza broke off with a choking sound, and Jase grabbed his empty ice cream dish. She emptied her stomach into it and then collapsed back in his hands. Her vision danced with streaks of light and her heart thudded unevenly in her tiny chest.

"What's going on?" Rayna asked, trying to glance back at them while still staying on the road.

"I don't know," Jase said. He sounded frightened. "Tierza just threw up. Do you think it was the ice cream?"

"No," the little girl muttered, trying to swallow away the bitter taste in her mouth. "Something else. It keeps getting worse."

"That's it," Rayna said. "We're taking her to a hospital as soon as we get to San Francisco. We're more than halfway."

The rest of the trip was very quiet and tense. Tierza drifted in and out of consciousness, and Jase never set her down, but held her in his hands and did his best to keep her warm.

She felt much better by the time they arrived at the edge of the huge city. Nikka used the GPS, trying to locate a hospital, and Tierza wiggled out of Jase's hands.

"I feel better," she announced.

"You should still see a doctor," Rayna said.

"Later, please? Can we go see the golden bridge?"

"Golden Gate Bridge," Jase said.

"Whatever. I'm much better now, Mom."

Rayna looked back with a bemused smile. "All right, Tierza. We'll go to the bridge first. But if you show any signs of being sick again, we'll go straight to the hospital. No matter how minor it seems."

"Okay. Thanks." The little girl sat down beside Jase and leaned against his leg.

"You're either crazy or really scared of doctors," he said.

Tierza smiled and closed her eyes, holding onto a fold of his jeans with both hands.

They drove another twenty minutes and then Tierza felt the car stop. She'd almost fallen asleep. Jase picked her up and she yawned as they climbed out of the car.

They were parked near the water, at the south end of the bridge. Tierza gazed up at the beautiful, towering structure, her mouth falling open a little as she stared.

"There it is," Jase said. "We could walk across it, if we want to."

"We did that when you were four or five years old," Nikka said. "And you wet your pants in the middle."

Jase poked his sister's arm and she jumped away with a giggle.

"Sadly we can't climb up to the tops of the towers," he said, turning his attention back to Tierza. "I've wanted to do that for as long as I can remember."

"You're crazy," Nikka said. She grinned and poked him back in the shoulder.

They stood for a moment and watched the bridge, with all the roaring traffic flowing back and forth across it. Tierza moved her gaze to the huge expanse of water. It frightened her a little, though she wasn't sure why.

"The San Francisco Bay," Jase said. "And out that way is the ocean. You can't see the end of the ocean, because the other side is so far away."

She didn't remember what an ocean was. That was strange. She knew cars and all sorts of other things, but not the ocean?

"What is that?" she asked.

"The ocean? It's just a whole lot of water. Like a huge, gigantic puddle."

"Oh."

Nikka coughed and covered her mouth with one hand. "Puddle," she murmured, shaking her head.

They stood for a moment longer, until Nikka yawned and headed back to the car.

"Now what?" Tierza asked.

Rayna looked at them and shrugged. "We're looking for someone as small as you, right?"

"Yes." She blinked up at the overcast sky. It had been so clear in Fresno, she thought it would be nice here as well. "Maybe they'll see me and come out from where they hide."

"Or maybe Philip was lying," Jase suggested.

"I told you, I don't think so." Tierza shuddered at the recollection. "He wasn't trying to impress me. He was just talking."

"Either way," Rayna said, "I think it's time to forget our worries and have a picnic."

They took the cooler and sat down in the grass. The green blades came almost up to Tierza's waist, so Jase put his hat on the ground upside down for her to sit on.

She ate a little piece of banana, but hardly more than two bites. Her stomach was still irritated, and she didn't want to make herself sick again and have to go to the hospital. Not when she was so close to finding out who she was.

Was she really so close? Maybe Jase was right; Philip was lying, and she only wanted to believe him. Maybe she was a freak, a one-of-a-kind creature...

But no, she remembered her father, and she remembered that she had a family. She must have come from somewhere in San Francisco, because Jase's box came from this city.

A strong breeze from the ocean blew over them, mussing up Nikka's loose hair, and Tierza shivered. She still wore her blue jacket, because no matter how warm it got, she always felt cold in just her thin shirt.

Jase finished eating and picked up Tierza and his hat. He set her on his knee and donned the hat, and they sat there watching Rayna and Nikka finish their sandwiches.

"You eat too fast," Nikka said, poking Jase in the ribs.

His stomach gurgled loud enough for Tierza to hear, and he grinned.

"Are we just going to sit here until something shows up?" Nikka asked.

"You have any better ideas?" Jase asked.

"No, I just—"

"Look!" Tierza shouted. She stood up on Jase's leg and pointed at the bridge.

The sun shone through a gap in the clouds, and now the entire area was flooded with light. The red color of the bridge turned to a brilliant shimmering gold.

"What are we looking at?" Nikka asked.

"The bridge. It's all golden."

They were too quiet, and Tierza looked up at Jase. He was frowning. Confused.

"What's wrong?" she said. "Can't you see? It's bright gold and sparkly."

The boy blinked. "Uh...sure."

She crossed her arms and glared at the bridge. "You can't see it? The sun just came out and—"

"Tierza," Rayna cut in, "the sun didn't come out."

The little girl stood stunned, and she looked up and shaded her eyes against the bright light.

There were two fiery orbs in the sky. One still hiding behind the thin clouds.

"Tierza?"

She felt a violent shiver go up her back, and she fell off Jase's leg. She closed her eyes and convulsed when she hit the ground, and when she opened them again, the second sun was gone and everything seemed very dim.

"Jase, pick her up. Nikka, pack our stuff. It's time to get that girl to a hospital."

Tierza rolled over and moaned just as the boy's fingers closed around her. Her skin was suddenly very sensitive, burning where his cold fingers touched. He carried her back to the car, and as she stared up into the sky she saw a winged figure streak over the bridge and into a grove of trees.

Unless she was imagining things, it was human-shaped. Winged and human-shaped. And small—just about her size.

"Stop!" she cried. "Don't...go..."

Her breath caught in her throat and her heart skipped more than one beat. They all jumped in the car and headed into the city, Nikka shouting out directions to the hospital while staring at the GPS, Rayna driving too fast, and Jase doing his best to make the little girl comfortable in his icy-cold fingers.

After a few minutes, her heartbeat evened out, her breathing became normal, and she started sobbing.

"Don't worry," Jase said. "We're taking you to a hospital."

"I saw...a little person. With wings." Tierza took a deep breath and it all burst out again as she cried.

"It's okay. We can go back later."

"No, now. Go back now—"

"Here's the hospital," Nikka shouted. "Mom! Turn here!"

The car swung around so fast that Jase's cheek squished into the window.

"There aren't any parking spaces here," Rayna said.

"Keep going. We'll probably have to park in the underground garage."

"How's our tiny girl doing?" Rayna asked over her shoulder.

"Breathing better," Jase said. "But she's crying."

"Father," Tierza gasped. "I need to...find..."

Nikka put away the GPS and twisted around in her seat. "What's she saying?"

"Something about her dad."

Tierza calmed and almost managed to stop crying. "Sorry," she whimpered. "I'm sorry."

"I wonder if Dad would know anything about little people," Nikka said.

"Probably not," Rayna snapped, a little too quickly. The car stopped and she switched it off.

"It's worth a try, at least."

"I don't know about that."

Tierza looked up at Nikka. "Who are you talking about?"

"My dad is a biology professor," she said. "He lives over in Oakland."

"He's my dad too," Jase added, a little crossly.

"Of course. But you were really little when he left."

"So? Doesn't matter."

Rayna groaned. "Kids! Stop arguing. That's pointless."

"Sorry."

They fell silent and spilled out of the car, and Tierza could feel the mood change. There was something about this father of theirs that bothered them.

Was he anything like her father? She still could hardly remember what he was like. Only that he'd tried to help her and eventually gave up. Could there ever be a good reason for a father to give up on his own daughter?

Chapter Twelve

Father

Jase hid Tierza under his coat as they ran to the emergency room. He figured there was no point in letting everyone see her. Just the doctor would be best, since doctors were well experienced with keeping secrets.

The young man at the desk just inside the entrance asked them what their emergency was. Jase looked at his mother and sister.

"Poisoning," Rayna said.

"With what?" the young man asked.

"We don't know, that's the problem."

"And who's poisoned here?"

Rayna glanced at Jase. He took the cue and wavered on his feet, giving a horrible rasping cough. The young man behind the desk nodded and told them to wait a minute.

When he came back, he motioned for them to follow him, and they went down a hallway to a small room. A balding man with glasses met them there, along with a cute nurse. Well, Jase thought she was cute. In fact, she looked a little bit like Tierza.

They all went into the room and Jase sat down on the edge of a bed.

"What happened here?" the doctor said.

"Mr...Franklin," Rayna said, peering at his nametag. "Can we talk to you? Just you, alone?"

The doctor looked bemused but he nodded and motioned the nurse out of the room.

"Doc," Jase said, "you're sworn to secrecy, all right?"

"What's this all about?"

Jase pulled Tierza from under his jacket and held her up in both hands. She gripped his fingers and stared with wide green eyes.

The doctor took off his glasses and wiped them with his shirt, but no doubt he saw the same thing when he put them back on.

"Holy anesthetic!" he said. "What is that?"

"Her name is Tierza, and she's been sick, but we don't know why."

Dr. Franklin took the little girl gently in his hands and peered at her. "But what is she?"

"We don't know," Jase said. "Will you just check her out and make sure she isn't dying? We're still trying to figure out what she is."

"Jason," Rayna murmured. "Don't be rude."

"Sorry."

Jase stared at Tierza. She was trembling. Of course. The last doctor who'd handled her wasn't very nice.

"Mister...uh, Doctor Franklin," he said, "can you be real careful with her? She gets scared of being handled and poked and stuff like that."

The doctor nodded absently and laid Tierza on the counter. "Sure, kid."

They all watched as Franklin examined the little girl, who endured it in silence though she looked terrified. Jase moved to the counter and let her hold onto his little finger. She seemed a little calmer after that. Up close he could see that her skin was flushed and dripping sweat. Whatever was wrong with her, it was getting worse.

The examination seemed to stretch on forever, and included taking a sample of blood, which Tierza got through with her eyes shut, and she gave only a brief squeak.

Jase and his mother and sister only spoke to answer Franklin's questions. Then at last the doctor straightened, holding the syringe up to the light.

"What do you think?" Nikka asked. "Is it very bad?"

"Some sort of poisoning," Franklin said. "But I've never seen symptoms quite like these. Granted, it might be different for a...small...um..."

"Person," Jase said.

"Yes. Well, I can run some tests on the blood, but I'm not optimistic about finding the poison."

"Can you give her anything?" Nikka asked.

"Not without knowing what to give. Treatments for poisons are often very specific. Antidotes and all that.

Considering that I've never before seen a tiny person like this, I really have no idea what could poison her."

Jase picked up Tierza and cradled her in his hands. She was limp and unresponsive now, still sweating and hot.

"How long will it take to run tests?" Rayna asked.

"Give me twenty minutes. I'll check for the common poisons that could cause these reactions."

Doctor Franklin went out, and Jase plopped down on the edge of the bed.

"Is she going to die?" he murmured, and tears stung his eyes.

Rayna laid a hand on his shoulder, and for a moment she didn't say anything. Then she sighed. "I hope not, Jason. I really hope not."

Tierza woke from her feverish sleep a little less than half an hour later, in time to hear the doctor's disappointing news. He found nothing harmful in her blood. Nothing at all, though there were more tests for extremely rare substances that could be done. He told them they should come back tomorrow at one p.m. and he would run some tests overnight.

They were very quiet all the way to the car. Jase held Tierza under his jacket again, but she could hear him sniffling. Then they got in the car and he brought her out. She stared up at him as he set her on the seat and put his belt on.

"Jase?" she said in an extra small voice.

"Hmm?"

"If I die...what will you do with me?"

He took a deep breath, and she thought she saw a trace of dread on his face, but he hid it well.

"Bury you in a pretty box, I think," he said very quietly.

"But we won't let you die without a fight," Nikka added.

"Mom," Jase said, leaning forward, "let's go see Dad. Maybe he'll have some ideas."

"I don't know..."

Nikka joined in. "Please? I want to see Dad anyway."

Rayna sighed. "All right. I suppose I can survive that."

Tierza was strong enough now to sit up on her own, but she had a feeling she wouldn't fully recover this time. Or ever. Her heart was having more trouble than before, and she knew. She was dying.

But what had happened? It must have been lost with the rest of her memories. Unless the problem was that she wasn't getting the right food.

No, she always felt better when she got food. She was poisoned, at some point before she woke up in the mailbox.

Did someone try to kill her? She remembered what her father had said in her flashback. *Already I'm defying the Court by not killing you on sight.*

Somebody at least wanted her to die.

Tierza clenched her jaw as she started to cry. She leaned up against Jase's leg, like before, but nothing could banish the dread of dying. It crept through her whole body like a dark, icy shadow, making her sick with fear.

Jase put his hand around her and she clung to his fingers and pressed her face into the soft crook of his knuckle. He was so big and resilient, and she was so fragile, but he couldn't protect her from something that would kill her from inside.

The car stopped after about half an hour and Tierza looked up. They were parked in front of a small but nice house, painted green with dark brown trim.

"Yuck," Nikka said. "I liked the blue paint job better."

"Dad is getting a little too crazy about 'going green'," Jase said as he climbed out of the car.

They went to the front door and Rayna rang the bell. After a few uncomfortable moments, a man with bed hair that stuck up at least four inches from his head answered the door. His hair was thick, just beginning to gray around the edges, and his face was peppered with a few days' worth of uneven beard growth. And his clothes...they were the sort of green you find in the jungle, an exotic mingling of various bright shades. Greener than even Tierza's own bright eyes.

"Rayna!" the man exclaimed. "And Nikka, Jason...this is a surprise. Come in!"

He didn't seem to notice the tiny face that looked out at him from Jase's pocket.

They filed past him into a dark hallway. The lights were on, but they were 'energy saver' bulbs that hardly put out enough illumination to distinguish colors. Once they were inside, the man's clothes looked dull.

"What brings you all to San Fran?" he asked.

"Some unusual business," Rayna said. "And Rod, we won't stay long."

He waved his hand at her and led them into a living room. It was lighter there, having the advantage of a large window. Rod brushed stacks of magazines and other mail onto the floor so they could sit down on wicker chairs. Model helicopters and airplanes of various sizes and shapes cluttered the shelves on the walls. A red and white sign by the window read *In case of natural disaster, use helicopter.*

Then Jase held out Tierza. "Before you ask, Dad," he said, "no, we don't know what she is, and her name is Tierza Velvet."

Rod nodded. "I'd say she's a faerie, except she doesn't have wings. Now, faerie is just the human term. I believe they call themselves the 'Ludic.' But since she doesn't have wings...I don't know."

"Dad, you know about tiny people?" Nikka asked.

Tierza glanced at Rayna and Nikka, who looked as surprised as the little girl felt.

"Of course I do. I wouldn't be much of a biologist if I didn't, would I?"

Jase scratched his head. "Well, uh…"

"Can I see you closer, Tierza?" Rod asked.

Tierza started trembling, and Jase held her back as his father donned a pair of round spectacles.

"Hey, I'll be very gentle. I've talked to your kind—the winged version at least. Trust me, you aren't just another creature to study. Not to me."

She didn't feel any better, but Jase handed her over

and Rod set her down on the coffee table.

"I'm a biologist," he said, "but that doesn't mean I cut up every new creature I see. Come on now, keep that chin up. Where did you come from? Without any wings, I wonder if you're not from the same place as the other faerie I've talked to."

"How many have you seen?" Jase asked.

Rod looked over his glasses at his son. "Just one. I'd been convinced of their existence for a while, and I met him over by the Golden Gate Bridge when I was searching for an entrance to their world. But that's another story. Anyway, he told me his daughter was in some trouble and if I ever saw her, would I make sure she was safe? He also said she'd die within two weeks, and the time is up on Monday, so I've been looking all over trying to find her. I even painted my house green, because it's a color that supposed to make faeries feel safer."

Safer? Tierza didn't feel safer at all. She bit her lip and trembled, feeling like she was on the brink of remembering. Two weeks...a daughter dying...

"Where did he come from?" Nikka asked. Everyone was fascinated by this new information, and even Rayna leaned forward and fixed her gaze on Rod.

"Apparently the land where they live is…er, not really in this dimension. There's sort of a hole, a portal if you will, that opens up above the Golden Gate Bridge. This faerie man says they don't use it much, because the humans are rarely gracious to their kind."

"What's his name?" Tierza asked.

"Josiah Aileron. I wonder…do you know him?"

She blinked. Did she?

Josiah Aileron.

A terrible ache pounded in her tiny head. Images began to flash across her vision. Sounds. Words.

Memories.

Then it all came rushing back, putting her flashbacks in context. She remembered everything.

Chapter Thirteen

The Crime

Three weeks earlier, Jera Aileron left her family's house and stretched her wide, feathered wings in the morning sunlight. She took a deep breath, closed her eyes, and smiled up at the blazing yellow orb.

It was a perfect day for flying. She took a little run and then skipped into the air, opening her eyes as the ground shot away from her bare feet and her wings carried her into the sky. A few white feathers drifted to the ground in front of the house, like permanent snowflakes on the grass.

Her parents didn't know where she was going. They might ask when she got back, but she was old enough now. Nobody but herself was responsible for her actions.

She'd turned five years old a week ago. It meant that she was no longer a child, and could begin courting. The expected lifespan of the Ludic was twenty-five years, unlike the humans' seventy-five. Jera couldn't imagine living for seventy-five years.

She never imagined that she had less than twenty-five more days to live, or barely twenty-five more minutes of a free life.

With no thoughts but happy ones for the future, Jera banked and descended in a slow spiral to land beside a crystal blue lake. She folded her wings and looked around, turning in a slow circle. The soft, damp grass tickled her feet and made a little shiver streak up her back.

She stopped. There he was. From behind a nearby tree, a young man emerged. His wings were golden, and even though white was the rarest color, she envied his shimmering feathers that soaked up the sunlight and reflected it for everyone to see.

"Faray," she said, a little breathless from her flight. Not to mention his dazzling looks.

He smiled, such a wonderful curve on his angelic face, and she just wanted to let him hold her, wrap his arms around her. But she restrained herself. A full embrace would not be appropriate yet.

This was Faray Wingletter, son of the Ludic King, and he loved *her*, a little white-winged nobody from an insignificant village. They'd met by chance just days ago, when he flew over her family's farm while hunting and landed for a rest. She'd given him a drink, shyly, knowing who he was. And then, what a glorious surprise, he'd asked her to meet him by this lake! Every morning and every evening they met, and talked, and she admired his wings and he said hers were far prettier. She said she would trade with him if they could, and he laughed at that idea.

Now she took a step forward, and so did the prince, and she reached out her hand so he could take it in the traditional courtship greeting, holding it between both of his hands for a moment before turning it over and letting it slide away. A symbol of how he might hold her in his heart now, but they weren't bound together yet. And they may never be, unless he dared to disobey his father, who wanted him to marry a highborn young lady from some other nation.

She suspected that Faray would much rather disobey his father than give her up, but for now they kept their love a secret. If it all fell apart, it would be easier to deal with if nobody else knew.

For him, maybe. Her heart would fall apart too, if that happened, and she didn't think it would go back together.

"Jera," he said, and his voice was as magnificent as the rest of him. "I haven't seen you under a blue sky before. Your wings are even prettier in the sun than in the rain."

She smiled and bowed her head as her cheeks heated up. "Yours are much more lovely. They shine like—"

"Like you do, perhaps," he said with a charming grin. "I love your wings because they are part of you."

She trembled a little, but kept her head bowed. It didn't seem right for her to look a prince in the eye.

Then she felt his hand under her chin. He'd never

touched anything other than her arms, and the feel of his fingers sent a hot flush over her skin.

Jera lifted her face, shaking now with the fierce passions that threatened to tear her apart.

"Why are you afraid?" Faray asked.

"I...well..." She gulped and twisted her fingers together behind her back, pressing them into her downy feathers. "You're the prince," she finished in a very small voice.

He laughed. Oh, how she loved that laugh!

"I'm not that much different from you," he said. "My heart wasn't built by the house I lived in, and my mind is my own. It doesn't matter who my father is. He'll understand."

Jera looked down again, pushing her chin past his fingers, and he sighed a little.

"Is something bothering you?" he asked.

"I want...to be free," she whispered. "I mean, we keep this a secret because your father won't approve. But I don't want it to be like that."

His finger traced a line down her jaw to her chin, and she shivered. She hoped he would do it again.

"If you want, I will tell my father."

"But what will he do?"

Faray leaned closer, and she smelled the soft scents of the palace that stuck to his bright scarlet tunic. "Whatever he does, he can't get in the way of love."

Before she could think of something to say, he took her hand and told her to come.

He led her back toward the water, but before they reached it, a large shape swooped down from the sky. Jera looked up and cried out in alarm, just as a tall, silver-winged man crashed down on Faray.

She scrambled back, and the prince went down in a heap. He threw off his attacker and leapt into the air, but the silver-winged man threw an object—a sharp, gleaming object—and it stuck into Faray's chest.

Jera screamed as the prince fell, golden wings crashing uselessly beneath him. The silver-winged one looked at her, then back at the prince. He stooped over Faray and pulled the object free, and then started toward her. A smirk spread across his face.

"Wrong place, wrong time," he said, shaking his head. "Poor girl."

She scooted backward, too terrified to get her wings out from under her. To terrified to even try to escape.

He raised his weapon, which was a short metal stake commonly used by farmers like her family. She collapsed onto her back, crushing her wings, and held her arms over her face.

"Please," she choked. "No...no..."

She expected to die as she lay there, frozen in terror. But then there was a distant sound, a shout, and she never felt the stake pierce her. Instead something was pressed into her hand and she heard the whoosh of wings.

A moment later she opened her eyes. Faray hadn't moved from where he fell, and she rolled over and scrambled to his side. She laid her head on his chest, but she could hear no heartbeat. His scarlet tunic was wet and dull with blood.

With his blood coating the side of her face, she sat back on her heels, hardly breathing, and stared at him. It felt like her own heart had stopped. A terrible ache spread through her chest.

There was a shout in the sky, and then four armed men dropped to the ground nearby. She could barely register that they were the royal guard. Her mouth remained closed, her eyes wide open, and she sat there motionless and silent.

Then the guards surrounded her and one grabbed her wings and heaved her to her feet. She winced as she lost a few feathers. Only then did she realize she still held the stake. The one that had killed the prince.

They wrenched it from her hand and pinned her arms and wings down until they got a length of rope wrapped around her. She vaguely wondered why she said nothing. But Faray was dead. She could think of nothing else. The shock was too much.

They carried her to the capitol, along with Faray's body. During the entire trip she didn't say a single word, and the guards didn't speak to her. She finally started crying, when they were in the air, and the tears dripped from her cheeks to fall through the wind like raindrops on this perversely sunny day.

They set her down outside the king's hall, and then led her in. One stood on each side of her, and the other two carried the prince's body between them. So Jera was brought, still crying, into the presence of the king.

He was a tall, stern man, with wings as golden as his son's. When he saw them, though, all the sternness fell away and she could see for a moment the father in him recognizing his son's body. He stepped forward, and swept his gaze from Faray over to her. She flinched as the hardness returned to his eyes.

"What happened?" the king asked. His voice was strained.

"Your son slipped away from our protection," one of the guards said. "We didn't find him until he was gone. This girl was beside him, holding the weapon that killed your son."

At this Jera blinked and shook off the blanket of shock that still weighed her down. "I didn't do it!" she cried.

The king stared for a moment.

"There was no one else there," the guard offered.

"Then what do you say?"

"It had to be her, my lord. Your son was hardly dead when we found them. He had been stabbed only moments before. There was no one else."

"No!" Jera shrieked. "There was...he was big, with silver wings, and he smirked, and he killed...oh please, I loved Faray!"

The king's eyes narrowed and he took a step forward. "How dare you insinuate that my son loved you? You're nothing but the daughter of a farmer, I can tell by your clothing. Did you seduce him? Tell me, what were your devious plans?"

She bowed her head and wept. "He loved me. He really did."

"She must be guilty," the king said, his voice as hard as his eyes. "Take her to the leech, and assemble the Court for a hearing."

Jera looked up at him, blinking away tears. "What?"

"Your flight is forfeit, young one. You are no longer one of us, no longer a free child of Ludic. You will be held in prison to await the Court's ruling on your sentence."

They dragged her away, and she fixed her mind on her last glimpse of Faray, her golden prince. But he would never hold her hand again. She would never get to feel his arms around her.

That last glimpse showed her what she'd lost— everything. And what she still had. Nothing.

Chapter Fourteen

Prison and Poison

A dark cell. A locked door. They left her there, left her to die. She was bleeding, crying, stripped of her spirit and her glory like a condemned criminal.

Jera Aileron had lost her wings. Her beautiful, wonderful, rare white wings. The leech had strapped her down and cut them off, and then applied a slimy concoction to close up the wounds. Already she could feel the stumps retreating, and soon she wouldn't be able to tell she ever had wings. The back of her simple dress was heavy with blood, and she slumped against the rough wall of her cell, too weak to do much more than whimper. Cold air came through the useless wing slits in her dress, to touch the sensitive skin on her back and make her shiver.

She fell into a deep, exhausted sleep for most of the first night, and awoke a little stronger. Her back was smooth already, and she stood up on shaky legs. She leaned forward too far without the weight of her wings and fell headlong on the stone floor. There was really no reason to get up. So she just lay there facedown and cried.

No one came to see her that first day. They shoved a small piece of overripe fruit and a shallow dish of warm water under the door for her meals, once in the morning and once in the evening. It was barely enough to sustain her, let alone regain her strength.

The blood soaking the back of her dress had dried, and it crackled whenever she moved. She didn't move often. There was no reason for it.

But there was plenty of reason to cry, so she did for most of the day. And late into the second night, when she couldn't sleep.

Jera drifted off for a couple hours, and awoke to the clank of the little flap in the bottom of the door as her morning meal arrived. She crawled over to it and gulped down the fruit. She drank the water slowly, washing each mouthful over her tongue before swallowing.

Josiah Aileron had a friend in the Court, a wise and aged man named Hector. When Hector heard that a girl with white wings had been arrested and awaited sentencing on charges of murdering the prince, he went and peered into her cell. He recognized her and sent a message to her father to come quickly.

That was how Josiah came to be standing outside his daughter's prison cell. The rest of his family remained at home. It had been hard enough for Hector to get permission for just the father to come.

The guard opened the door and Josiah stepped in, his friend just behind him. At first he barely recognized his daughter, without her wings and in the twilight of the cell. She lay on her belly on the floor, her face turned toward the door, as if she was trying to get a glimpse of the outside world through the crack at the bottom.

When Josiah knelt beside her and touched her empty back, her dress that was stiff with blood, she stirred and lifted her head. Their eyes met for a moment, and then she moistened her cracked lips.

"Father," she whispered.

Josiah couldn't speak. He hunched his shoulders and pulled her into his arms, as great hot tears rolled down his cheeks.

"I didn't do it," Jera murmured.

"What happened?" he finally asked.

"I'm sorry..." She paused, gathering the strength to go on. "I met the prince, and he was nice to me. He asked me to meet him by the lake. So we met there for a few days. He said he loved me."

At that Jera had to stop and sob into her father's chest for a moment before she could continue. "A man, big with silver wings, attacked and killed Faray. Then he put the weapon in my hand and flew away, and that's how the guards found us. I couldn't do anything, I was so scared."

Hector laid a hand on Josiah's shoulder. "Time to go," he said. "I'm sorry."

Jera clung to her father until he stood up and laid her back down. He watched her curl up on the floor, opened his mouth to say something encouraging, and found no words for it. So he closed his mouth and left the cell, and winced when the door clanged shut behind him.

"She seems to be telling the truth," Hector said as they walked slowly back to the Court House.

"Of course she is!" Josiah snapped. "My little Jera never lies."

"The problem is that the king has already decided her guilt. All the Court will do is decide a sentence for her."

Josiah stopped. "What? You mean she's already found guilty of murder? That's preposterous!"

"You should keep your voice down. Calling the king's decisions preposterous could make trouble for you."

A fresh tear ran down Josiah's cheek. "We're talking about my oldest daughter here. My first child! What punishment do you think they will choose?"

"Death is most likely..."

Josiah let out a choked sob.

"...but, as I am your friend, I think I can sway the Court to be more lenient."

"What's the best we can hope for?"

"Permanent banishment."

A week went by, and Josiah stayed in the capitol. He saw Jera a few more times, but never longer than a couple minutes. She kept saying she was sorry for not telling him about Faray. It broke his heart every time.

The Court picked up her case a week and two days after the day of the murder. Without Hector it would have been a quick decision—a public execution. But through clever arguing and sympathy he got them to consider the girl's family, her clean upbringing, and the possibility that she could be innocent.

"That is not relevant," the ancient Duce had said. "Whether she is innocent or not, the king has determined her guilt, and that is the law. All we must decide is her punishment."

And then the Court had broken out into argument again, because a few had sided with Hector early on, proposing that they should push for, at the most, just a prison sentence.

In the end, majority ruled and the result was less than satisfactory. Josiah took it surprisingly well. He had to sit down, and turned very pale, but he'd been preparing himself for this news all week.

"You are her father," Hector said then. "It is traditionally your place to administer the venom prick. I will go with you."

Josiah rose as if in a trance and followed Hector to a room in the leech's wing, where Jera lay strapped down to a table. She turned her head when they entered, and he saw that she was gagged, her soul-cutting emerald eyes blurred with tears.

He almost turned and left then, unable to endure seeing her like this. But he had to stay. He stood by her for a moment and stroked her hair, and then Hector stepped forward with a small needle. Jera looked at it, and then at her father, and he turned away.

"If you cannot do it, you can pass the responsibility to me," Hector said.

"No...I'll do it."

Hector watched his friend. "You seem to hesitate, and I understand that. But this has to be done, Josiah. The ruling has been passed. You cannot save her from her fate."

"I know." Josiah swallowed hard and his voice descended to barely above a whisper. "I know. If she must die like this, I want to have her life on my hands and on none other's."

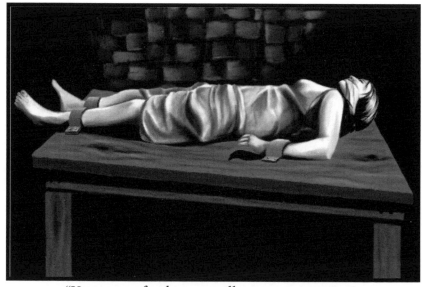

"You are afraid you will want revenge? I can understand. Here is the needle. Do it quickly while I watch."

Josiah took the needle and paused, running his hand through Jera's hair. "She's so young…"

"You are stalling," Hector said.

Josiah brushed some stray locks away from the side of her neck and winced as he stabbed the needle in. His hands shook and he dropped the deadly device on the floor. "There, I did it," he muttered. "See? But I'll never forget. She is beautiful, Hector. I wish she could have had a full life first."

"There is much pain ahead for this one. I am sorry, Josiah, I truly am. Be glad the ruling spared her from a worse fate. This is a merciful end, rather than some of the other punishments that could have been chosen."

Josiah bent over and kissed his daughter's forehead. "But there is no chance for pardon."

"No, there is not. The deed is done."

Josiah stared a moment longer, and then turned and left the room. Turned his back on his firstborn daughter.

Hector was wrong. This wasn't merciful. It gave her two more weeks to suffer before she died, rather than being publicly beheaded and having it over in an instant.

But he preferred this way, even though it pained him to admit it. She would be banished from the country, and he wouldn't have to see her die. If there was anything she wanted to do, she had two weeks to do it.

Such a short time for a life.

Chapter Fifteen

The Punishment

When Jera was brought before the Court to hear the official announcement of her fate, her father wasn't there. Hector got a moment alone with her beforehand and said that Josiah had gone home.

She was already dead to her father.

They had to carry her to the Court House, because her meager diet and loss of blood had left her barely able to walk. The effects of the prick she'd gotten the day before hadn't begun yet, but she'd lost so much weight that her skin was stretched over her ribs. She kept touching them, because they felt strange. She'd never been this thin before.

They put her in the center of the vast circular room, her hands and feet chained. She faced the Duce, who contorted his wrinkled face to match the severity of the words he intoned.

"Jera Aileron," he boomed. "The king has found you guilty of murder, and as such, we have been charged with determining your fate. You have been given a venom prick, which you must know will bring an end to your life after two weeks. For these two weeks you will be released, though you are banished from this country. You have three hours to leave, and if you are found within the borders after that time, you face instant death. Do you have any questions?"

She remained silent, and then two guards came and unlocked her chains. They led her out and threw her in the street.

Jera staggered to her feet and stumbled away, leaning against the wall of the Court House until she reached the corner, and then she somehow managed to stagger along on her own.

A sympathetic farmer took her for a beggar and tossed her a whole fresh redfruit. She sat down by the street to scarf it down, and it gave her enough strength to walk. Then she left the capitol and wandered along the paths of the vineyards outside its walls.

"I didn't do it," she cried, but nobody would hear her.

Her three hours were nearly up when she reached the nearest border of the country. Just over the line, there was a dirty little village inhabited by the Unwinged, people like her who had lost their wings and their freedom for crimes less serious than hers. It was a rough place, where women and children were little more than slaves, and the men were cruel.

Jera stood at the edge of the town until she worked up the courage to enter. When she did, she slunk along and tried to remain invisible among the grubby people.

Her dress was hardly fit to wear anymore, and when she saw a tinker's wagon she stopped and eyed a display of clothes made specially for the Unwinged.

She hid behind a corner and watched for her chance. When the tinker was alone and turned his back on the clothes, she dashed out and blindly grabbed an armful of clothing. Then she ran.

"Hey you! A thief! Stop her!"

Adrenaline pumped through her body with every footstep, and Jera fled through the mazelike alleys of the village until she was hopelessly lost. Lost, but alone. No one still pursued her, so she stopped and looked at her loot.

She picked out nice blue jacket, a pair of pants in the style of the humans, and a pink shirt. Looking around to make sure nobody was watching her, she quickly changed and left her old dress in a heap with the rest of the clothes she didn't need.

She wandered the alleys until dark, looking for a way out of the village. Once she came across a pair of shoes outside a doorway. They fit her perfectly, so she took them. She only had two weeks to live anyway. If they caught her stealing and executed her sooner, all the better.

The shoes felt strange. She'd never worn any before, since she'd grown up on a farm, running wild in bare feet before she could fly. And having wings made shoes hardly necessary anyway.

Eventually she was too exhausted to go on, so she crawled down a narrow, dark hole between an abandoned house and another one that had collapsed against it, and she fell asleep.

In the morning Jera woke early and continued her search for a way out of the village. She'd just stepped around the corner of a crooked building when someone grabbed her and threw her to the ground. She skidded on the rough surface and whimpered, instinctively curling up to protect herself.

"Hey, guys, I found the thief!"

Jera peered up at her attacker as he laid a foot on her side to hold her down. He was huge, at least fifteen inches tall, unwinged, and ugly. He smirked down at her and ground his heel into her gaunt ribs.

"We'll have to take them clothes back," he said. "They don't belong to you."

She grabbed his foot and yanked it off of her, and while he recovered his balance she scrambled to her feet. But she didn't get very far. Her attacker tripped her and then pounced and heaved her to her feet. He punched her belly and she doubled over, and the scream that she nearly got out turned into a breathless moan.

Three more men joined the first, and they shoved her back and forth, all taking turns beating her. She finally collapsed, bruised and only half-conscious, and the huge man stooped over her and grabbed her jacket and started to yank it off.

"Hey, you!"

He stopped and looked in the direction of the new voice. All four of them did.

Another young man sauntered up to them and stopped, standing by Jera's shoulder. She'd never seen a bigger faerie. He had to be at least sixteen inches tall, and his arms were thicker than her legs.

Her four attackers backed off a little. Jera lay tense and frozen, wondering how stupid it would be to try running away.

"This isn't your business, Carney," her ugly attacker said. "She's a thief. Stole them clothes, and we was hired to get 'em back."

Jera whimpered. Was the newcomer going to help her, or would he help her tormenters beat her and take her clothes?

Carney spoke in an even tone. "Tell me what the clothes are worth and I'll pay for them."

She started breathing easier, almost sobbing with relief. Somebody at least didn't want to hurt her.

"That isn't the deal—"

"Shut your mouth, Dray, or I'll shut it permanently. You just want an excuse to take the girl's clothes off. If you try that, I'll knock your head off."

Jera wondered if that was a literal threat.

Dray scowled, but held his hands up in surrender. "You wanna waste money on a worthless girl, that's your problem. The tinker wants fifty for the clothes."

Carney dug into his pocket and handed over a handful of golden coins. "Here's seventy-two. Three for each of you, and sixty for the tinker."

Dray took the money and started counting it.

"I'll be talking to the tinker later to make sure you gave him sixty," Carney said.

"And if not, you'll knock my head off. Yeah, I know."

Dray turned and shoved past his three friends, and they leered at Jera for a moment longer before following him.

Carney lifted her up and set her on her feet. She didn't even stand as high as his shoulder. She winced as he dusted her off, and when he let go, she backed away from him.

"What's your name?" he asked.

"Doesn't matter," she mumbled. And then she turned and ran. He didn't follow her.

Exhausted, bruised, and bleeding, Jera finally found the end of the maze-like village. Heedless of the Duce's death threat, she crossed the border into her own country again and headed toward her family's farm. She wanted to see them one last time, even if it meant she would die today.

Walking was so much harder and took a lot longer than flying. Jera tramped through the sparsely populated countryside for hours, growing weaker and trying to sustain her strength with wild berries and fruits, and sometimes food stolen from orchards, vineyards, and farms.

It was late afternoon when she finally saw her old home, and when she did she collapsed to her knees and just let her tears run for a few minutes. Then she forced herself to her feet and went to the door.

Josiah opened to her knock. He looked older somehow, and surprised.

"I wanted to see mother and all the children," Jera said. "Just one last time."

"They aren't here," he replied, looking her over with an expression she couldn't read.

"Where are they?"

There was a moment of silence.

Jera sagged against the doorframe. "I don't want to go!" she cried. "I want to come home and work on the farm, and eat mother's pie. I want to play with Torry and pick berries and teach the baby to fly—"

"You shouldn't have come back here," Josiah said. "Don't you know what will happen if they find you?"

"Father, I...please, can't you do anything?"

"I tried," he growled. "Believe me, I tried everything I could. Already I'm defying the Court by not killing you on sight."

"Father! I didn't do it!"

"I believe you. But nobody else does. I can't do any more without bringing trouble on myself and the rest of the family as well."

Jera stared into his troubled eyes. "You wouldn't even run away with me?"

He clenched his jaw. "I have your brothers and sisters and mother to look after. Should I take them all along to a similar fate? Look at me, Jera. I cried. I still cry. I hate this, but I'm trapped. You need to just go."

She turned and walked away, shoving her hands into her jacket pockets.

"Jera..."

She paused.

"I'm so sorry. I'd never turn you in. I just can't bear to see you get hurt."

She kept walking and didn't look back. "Selfish," she muttered to herself. "He doesn't want to see me get hurt, so I have to deal with it myself?"

As she trudged down the road, toward the wild lands she'd never been allowed to explore as a child, she heard shouts behind her.

"I saw Jera!"

"You did?"

"The murderess went that way! We'll track her down and have her head!"

Jera froze for a moment, and then took off running, sobbing so bitterly she could barely breathe. She left the path behind and fled into the forest, welcoming its savage wildness rather than the cruelty behind her.

After a while she heard a snarl, and realized her pursuers were getting closer. She scrambled under a small bush and crouched there, her breath coming in rapid, terrified bursts. Her heart raced so fast it was just a hum. Something was hunting her. She'd been turned away from her own home, and now they wanted to find her and hurt her.

She heard the sniffling of the tracking beast, and bolted out the other side of the bush with a strangled sob. An abrupt drop opened up in front of her and she tried to stop, but her momentum carried her over and she fell.

Jera shrieked as she plummeted through the air, and a whole new world opened up beneath her. The world of the humans. As a small child, she'd always wanted to visit this world, and she had studied it as much as she could. Cars, roads, skyscrapers—it all fascinated her.

But now she would get only a brief glimpse from the air before she hit the ground and broke all her bones, or hit the water and drowned.

Still screaming, she fell closer and closer to a huge red bridge that spanned the water. Then something closed around her body and she jerked to a stop. And started going back up.

She twisted around to see that she was in the claws of a giant feathered beast. A bird. This one had a hooked beak. What was it called? Eagle? If she weren't in its claws, she would be in awe of the magnificent bird.

Jera cried and struggled, not sure if it would be better to fall to her death or be eaten by a bird. The eagle ignored her and flew over the city. When it passed low over one of the skyscrapers, it dropped her and she crashed down into its nest.

Now she was surrounded by three hungry little eagles, each as tall as her and three times as heavy. They chirped excitedly and snapped at her, but she dropped to the bottom of the nest and they collided with each other.

Jera stared down through the woven sticks and grasses of the nest. There was a gap big enough for her to wriggle into, and like a frantic worm, she burrowed down out of reach of those greedy little beaks.

She finally tumbled out the side of the nest, scratched and bloody. The eagles screamed indignantly and she ran across the roof of the building.

And then, as she glanced behind her, empty space opened up beneath her feet and she fell again. This time nothing caught her, and she landed on a hard surface and nearly blacked out. All around her, things

were hissing and popping and slamming. The noise made her head hurt—or maybe it was the fall. When she touched the side of her head, her fingers came away bloody.

A large box sat beside her, and she crawled to it. With the last of her strength she climbed over the edge and fell in, where she curled up in the darkness and waited to die.

The box moved with a terrific jolt, and the top closed. The last thing she remembered before sleep took her was something large and heavy shifting inside the box and smashing her against the side with enough force to crack her ribs.

Chapter Sixteen

Hope

Tierza blinked and pressed her fists to the sides of her head. The memories whirled through her mind and made her dizzy.

"Tierza?" Jase said, picking her up. "What's wrong?"

"I remembered. Everything."

"Wait a minute," Rod said. "You're the daughter?"

Tierza nodded.

"No!" Jase cried. "She's dying?"

"Two days left," Rod said with a solemn nod.

"There's got to be a cure!"

"No," Tierza moaned. "There isn't. That's why they gave it to me."

"Who?"

"The Ludic Court," she muttered. "Yes, I'm a faerie, if that's what you want to call me. I lost my wings...no, they took them away. Nice white wings."

"Why would they do that?" Nikka demanded. "It's so cruel!"

Tierza swallowed and gritted her teeth, trying to drive away the throbbing pain in her head. She managed to sit up in Jase's hands. "They think I killed the prince."

"What happened?"

Tierza took a deep breath. "A lot of painful things."

Nobody said anything. She looked up at Jase and saw tears in his eyes. Rod wore a frown and chewed on the end of his glasses. Rayna and Nikka leaned forward in their chairs, looking like they were about to say something but the words got stuck in their throats.

"It's all right," Tierza whispered. "I'll just go..."

"What did you say?" Rayna asked.

"Don't worry," she said, a little louder. "My fate is already decided. All I want is for you to remember me."

Rod sat up straighter and put his glasses back on. "Of course we'll remember you."

"That's real comforting, Dad," Jase grumbled.

"Just listen. I have a friend who's a brilliant toxicologist. I'll bet he could examine your blood and find out what sort of poison you've got in you. Chances are we already have an antidote that could save your life."

"You think so?" Tierza's voice trembled and she gripped Jase's thumb. "Is there actually hope?"

"Of course! There'll be hope right up until you die—that is, if you die. You know what I mean."

"And he wonders why we couldn't get along," Rayna mumbled.

"I heard that," Rod said as he stood up. "Come along, people. It's time to draw some blood."

Tierza shivered and pressed her hand to the spot on her arm where Rachel Lindon's needle had gone in.

Rayna, Jase, and Nikka followed Rod through a maze of messy rooms to an incongruously spotless laboratory. Scientific instruments were lined up and categorized on one counter, and jars of preserved specimens lined another. Tierza stared at the face of a dead frog, and her stomach lurched.

At least Miss Lindon's animals had been alive.

"How do you keep this room so tidy?" Rayna asked.

Rod glanced back from the cupboard he was searching through. "I can't stand a disorganized workspace."

"Dad, what about the rest of your house?" Nikka gestured at the doorway. "It's a dump."

"That's space for playing and lazing around. This is workspace. Besides, don't you think that the mess out there makes you better appreciate the organization in here?"

"About as much as being in Antarctica can make you better appreciate the Sahara Desert," Jase said.

Rod turned to face them and screwed a thin needle onto a tiny syringe. Tierza started quaking in Jase's hands.

"I don't think she's okay with this," the boy said.

"I doubt she's okay with dying on Monday," Rod replied. "Now set her on the counter."

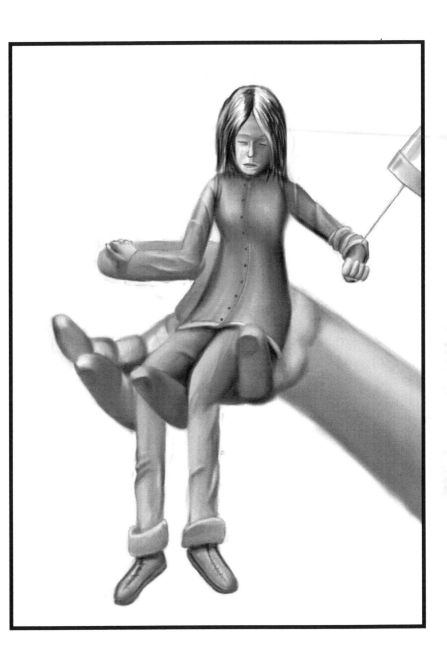

"No!" she cried. "Let him hold me."

"The faerie doesn't like needles, eh? Very well. Hang onto her, Jase. Don't drop the little thing."

"Her name's Tierza," Jase said.

"I do remember that. Oh, come on, Tierza, it isn't going to hurt you."

"She had a traumatic experience earlier this week with needles."

Tierza scowled up at them. "Just hurry up before I can't stand waiting any more!"

Rod held her arm between two fingers and applied a local anesthetic to her wrist. Then he stabbed the needle in and her stomach lurched. She had to look away as her blood oozed into the syringe.

"That should be enough," Rod said as he withdrew the needle. "Yes, quite enough. I'll call up Howard and see when we can drop by. Excuse me."

He left the room and Tierza curled up in Jase's hands, holding her wrist and trying to rub away the strange numb feeling.

"Does it hurt?" he asked.

"No."

"You're really pale."

She shuddered and closed her eyes. "Well yes. Dying isn't very good for my health."

Rod left a few minutes later to run the blood sample over to his friend Howard. The brilliant toxicologist lived a few blocks away, so Rod was back in fifteen minutes.

"Howard will call when he finds out anything about the poison," he told them.

"Now what?" Jase asked.

"We wait. Tell me about what you've been doing recently, kids. We haven't talked for a while."

They sat down in the living room again while Nikka and Jase regaled their father with stories of Tierza, hardly mentioning anything else.

"You've gotten pretty attached to the faerie," Rod remarked.

Tierza curled up on an empty chair and didn't say much. She sympathized with Rayna, who hung back in the doorway and listened. Somehow they were both outsiders in this group, talked about almost as if they weren't there.

Jase was giving an account of how he got beat up by Philip so Tierza could escape when movement by the window caught the little girl's eye. She lifted her head and squinted into the sunlight.

There it was again—a small, winged figure. The wings were sky-blue. A lump formed in her throat and she sat up.

"...so then I tried to punch his nose again," Jase said, "but his friends got hold of me—"

"Father?" Tierza said.

Rod looked up, finally noticing the soft tapping on the window. "Oh! It's Josiah. I'll let him in."

He left the room and Tierza heard the front door open. Then it closed. Rod made some sort of greeting, and Josiah Aileron darted into the room. He landed on the coffee table and stared at Tierza.

She slumped in her seat and looked back at him. Her strength was draining away. With two days left to live, she would only get weaker.

Jase and Nikka were as quiet as their mother, and even Rod didn't say anything when he entered the room again and sat down.

"Jera," the faerie man said. That was all. His chest heaved and his wings quivered with exhaustion.

She didn't reply. She just closed her eyes and listened to her own breathing. In...out...in...cough...gasp...

Her eyes popped open and she shook with ragged coughing.

"My daughter," Josiah said, looking like he was going to cry.

"Don't...call me that," she wheezed between coughs.

A tear rolled down his cheek. "I never thought I'd see you again."

"Why would you want to? You didn't want to see me hurting. Well I'm hurting now. You should leave."

Josiah sat down and bowed his head for a moment, and then he met her gaze. "The king is dead. We are at war with a fierce army that came from the east. Nobody knows who they are, but they're strong, and every man and boy able to lift a weapon is joining the battle. Torry left home yesterday."

Tierza's eyes widened. "To fight? And you let him?"

"He is almost a man. It's his decision."

She clenched her jaw and began to sob. "Not Torry..."

"If men don't risk their lives in battle, innocent women and children may die afterward."

"What happened to the king?" Tierza's voice was hardly more than a whisper.

"He was killed by a tall, silver-winged man. The guards trapped the assassin but he committed suicide rather than be captured."

"Does the Court know I'm innocent now?"

Josiah sighed. "They're too busy trying to keep the country together. I doubt they have even thought of you."

"But you?"

"Jera, I've thought of you constantly. Giving in to the Court's ruling was the hardest thing I ever did, but I thought I had to do it for the sake of my family. You understand that, don't you?"

"Sure." She lay down on her side and blinked as tiny tears dripped on the seat cushion. "You should go back and be with Mother and the children."

Josiah flew from the table to her chair and knelt beside her. "You are one of my children," he whispered. "I tried to let you go but I couldn't. Nothing can change the fact that you're my daughter." He suddenly slumped and began to cry. "Forgive me. I wanted to fight for you, but I didn't. I should have. I couldn't...it tore me to pieces, Jera. I froze with fear until it was too late. Please, forgive me!"

The humans had watched and listened in spellbound silence during the whole conversation, but now Jase stood up.

"Is there any way we could get to this faerie land?" he asked.

"Jason, are you crazy?" Nikka asked.

A wide smile spread across Rod's face. "No he isn't. He's got an idea there. Josiah, what sort of weapons do your enemies have?"

The faerie man stood and turned to face them. "Swords, spears, a few explosives. Why?"

"I was just wondering if it would make a difference if you had three or four humans on your side."

Rayna stepped into the room. "No!" she snapped. "I'm not sending my children to some other world into the middle of a war."

"Aw, Mom," Jase said. "Their swords must be like toothpicks. And explosives? Firecrackers, Mom. We'll be almost invincible."

"I think he's right," Nikka said. "And how often do we get the chance to go to another world?" She stood up and put one arm around her brother's shoulders. "It might be crazy, but count me in."

"How will you get there?" Josiah asked. "The portal is in the sky."

Rod winked. "Leave that to me."

Chapter Seventeen

The Helicopter

After a short argumentative discussion about visiting the faeries' world, Jase convinced Tierza to tell them what had happened to her. So she told them the story in as short a time as she could, feeling a little hesitant to bare every personal detail.

Howard called twenty minutes later with discouraging news. He couldn't find any sort of poison in the blood sample, and he'd already run every test that could be done before Monday.

Tierza shivered when Rod gave them the news in a flat voice. It brought the previously excited conversation to a painful halt.

"So she's going to die anyway?" Jase asked, sounding very young and scared in the solemn moment.

Nobody answered. Josiah squeezed his daughter's shoulder, and she closed her eyes and sighed.

"No cure," she muttered.

"I'm so sorry," Josiah said in a choked voice. "I can't believe...I let this happen."

Tierza swallowed, fighting back the tightness in her throat. "Me neither," she whispered.

Then she felt gentle fingers around her, and opened her eyes enough to see that Nikka was picking her up.

"So Dad," Nikka said with a sniff, "how will we get into the faeries' world?"

"Oh, right," Rod said. "Come out to the yard with me. I'll show you."

Rod's backyard was large for such a small city house, and a helicopter sat in the middle of it.

"Whoa, Dad, when did you get that?" Jase asked.

"Recently," Rod said. "It seats only two, so we'll have to take multiple trips."

"I still haven't agreed to this," Rayna grumbled.

Jase grabbed her hand. "Think about it this way. You have a chance to go to a whole new world that no human has ever seen!"

Nikka stayed silent and stared down at the wingless faerie in her hands. Tierza watched Josiah fly, as she coughed and dreamed of the days when she had wings. She could launch herself into the sky whenever she wanted, and feel the wind rush over her body and give her wonderful little chills.

Josiah landed on Rod's shoulder. "I don't know if the portal is big enough for your helicopter," he said.

"We'll just have to find out then, won't we?" Rod opened the door and climbed into the cockpit. He looked back. "Rayna, this is an adventure rarer than finding unfossilized dinosaur bones in Siberia. And we're doing it to help people. Twelve-inch-tall people with wings, maybe, but they're still people. And they need help. Well yes, of course they do, that's why we're doing it to help them, but—"

"Rod!" Rayna cut in. There was just a hint of a smile on her face, and she looked at her children. "I get the point."

"Will you let the kids go? It was their idea. Can we agree on this for once and trust God for their safety?"

Rayna stared at Jase for a moment, and then Nikka, and then she sighed and nodded. "All right. But first, get some sort of protection. Coats, goggles..."

Jase and Nikka ran inside and dug through Rod's closet. They came up with two old leather coats, a couple pairs of scratched safety glasses, and then Jase dragged out some tennis rackets.

"What do you think?" he asked his sister, swinging one like a baseball bat.

She took another and stared at it. "For fighting faeries? Brilliant."

They tucked the coats and rackets under their arms and went back outside as the helicopter was just starting up.

"Take me first," Nikka said, stepping forward with Tierza.

"What?" Jase whined. "Why do you get to—"

"This isn't the time to be a little boy, son," Rod said, leaning out of the helicopter. "This is a time to be a man. If your sister wants to go first, will you be courteous and let her?"

Jase nodded. "Sorry, Dad, you're right. Go ahead, Nikka."

Rod started flipping switches as Nikka climbed into the other seat. She tucked Tierza into a fold of her shirt and pulled the door shut, twisting the handle to latch it.

Tierza was barely able to move. Her stomach and head were agitated, and she clung to the warm fabric that enveloped her, like a baby would cling to its favorite blanket.

"You okay?" Nikka asked.

Tierza could only moan. She stared through her fuzzy vision at Rod, as he continued to get the helicopter ready for flight.

"Rayna!" Rod shouted over the noise of the accelerating engine. "Take Jason in your car and meet me by the Golden Gate Bridge. Josiah, get over here."

The faerie man darted across the lawn and into the cockpit. He landed on Nikka's knee and crawled close enough to hold Tierza's hand.

Rod closed his door and the helicopter blades sped up, starting to make the distinctive chop-chop sound.

Nikka put on the copilot's headset after watching her father don his own. She kept her hands away from the controls, though, and focused on making sure Tierza stayed comfortable.

Then the helicopter rose, and everything else dropped out of sight. Tierza's stomach lurched and she clenched her jaw, trying not to throw up.

"I'm going to swing north," Rod shouted over the noise. "There's a lot of air traffic around the lower half of the San Francisco Bay. Two international airports, three smaller ones, and a U. S. Army base all within a thirteen-mile radius. It's crazy. You wouldn't believe how many birds are hit by airplanes around here."

"Hmm," Nikka said, staring out the window with a pale, sick expression.

"Yes, I do have a license to fly these things," Rod said. "No need to look so disturbed about it."

The helicopter was so small that it bounced around like a giant housefly in the sky. Rod was perpetually yanking the control stick around when gusts of wind hit them, and the resulting ride was sickening.

Tierza could barely keep from gagging. She ended up putting a couple of her fingers in her mouth and sucking on them in an effort to keep herself from throwing up.

"There's the bridge," Rod announced at last.

Josiah let go of his daughter's hand and looked out. "How will you know where the portal is?" he asked.

"That's what I need you for, little man with wings. You'll have to go out there and lead me in. Fly up through the very center of the portal, and I'll follow you when you vanish."

"You will only have a few moments before it closes," Josiah said. "I can try to keep it open from the other side but it will be hard."

"Just do your best. And stay away from the chopper blades. I'd hate to have to add you to the aircraft-caused fatality list."

Rod opened his door a crack, holding the helicopter relatively steady, and Josiah fluttered across and dived out, keeping his wings folded until he cleared the rough downdraft. Then he swooped up and sped out in front of them.

Tierza lay limp in Nikka's hands and stared through the glass. Her heart was so weak she kept thinking it had stopped, and every breath was hard. Her father was out there trying to save the country that had rejected his own daughter. And all she could do was lie here and die.

"Nikka," she murmured, "I'm so cold."

"What?" Nikka hunched over and put her ear close to the little girl's face.

"Help," Tierza mumbled, barely aware of her own words. "I didn't do it. Don't leave me...please, Father, please!"

"Hang on, Tierza," Nikka cried. "You still have two days left. You can't die yet!"

Then the little girl felt something slipping away, something that wanted to soar free. She wondered if that was her soul, eager to leave her body and start a new life without the pain of this one.

The air left her lungs in a long, contented sigh and she closed her eyes. She felt one last beat of her heart before consciousness left her.

And then silence.

Jase sat in the passenger seat as Rayna drove, intimidated by her frowning silence. He wished Tierza was there, so he'd at least have someone to talk to. Someone who wasn't...Mom.

He still couldn't believe Tierza was dying. Just a week ago he'd taken her out of the mailbox, and sure, she was injured and terrified. But at the time he never would've imagined that she was poisoned and already dying.

As they drove, he sometimes caught glimpses of the helicopter in the distance. Nikka was going to be the first human to set foot in the faeries' land, as far as they knew. He tried not to let anyone else know, but he was jealous. It was even worse when he had to keep worrying that his mom would change her mind and not let him go at all.

He amused and distracted himself by imagining what this new world would be like. He imagined faeries building their cities in the branches of huge trees, and butterflies mingling with the little winged people.

Then he envisioned a miniature version of his own world, with cars and skyscrapers, and the only real difference, besides the size, were the people's wings.

Jase couldn't wait to see for himself what it was really like.

Finally Rayna got off the freeway and parked near the water, at the same spot where they'd eaten their picnic lunch. It was evening now, and they hadn't eaten dinner yet. Jase's stomach growled and he pressed his hand to it.

The helicopter was hovering a short distance from the bridge, and then it started moving slowly. Rayna and Jase climbed out of the car and stood side by side in the grass, watching the small craft navigate the vast gray sky.

As they watched, it stopped moving forward and rose straight up. Slowly, inching upward like a cautious insect. Jase realized his fists were clenched and sweaty, and he opened his hands and wiped them on his pants.

"I never thought I'd be seeing this," Rayna said.

Jase glanced up at her. "Well, I'll bet you never thought faeries were real," he said.

"Hmm."

"Why don't you and Dad get back together?"

Rayna was silent for a moment. Then she cleared her throat. "It didn't work the first time."

"Sure it did. It worked for more than ten years."

There was no response. The boy shrugged and turned his attention back to the helicopter.

Then it vanished. Like a projected image suddenly switched off, it was gone. Jase heard his mother's breath catch, and he almost started jumping up and down.

"They did it!" he shouted. "They're in the faeries' world now!"

Chapter Eighteen

In the Land of Faeries

Nikka barely noticed when they rose through the ground of another world. She had her ear pressed to Tierza's chest, trying to detect a heartbeat, or breathing, or any sign of life. But the helicopter made too much noise.

Rod set the craft down in a large field and shut off the engine. Nikka's breath caught as she stared out the windows and saw her surroundings, a world on a tiny scale. Everything was small. The trees, the grass, the mountains.

For people twelve inches tall, it would look normal.

Rod opened his door and Josiah flew into the cockpit.

"You made it!" the faerie gasped. "I was afraid you would crash. It was close; the portal almost closed too soon. It sometimes opens on its own when the weather in both worlds is similar, but today it's very stubborn."

"Climb out now, Nikka," Rod said. "I'm going to get your mom and brother."

She nodded and stepped out onto the fine, hair-like grass. There was a sky overhead—a different one than in the world below. This place was somehow a completely separate world. She felt so big that she might be able to touch the puffy white clouds.

She ran a safe distance from the helicopter as the blades started spinning again. And she watched her feet, feeling like she didn't belong here, until she stopped at the edge of a forest. The tallest trees were only double her height.

Tierza still lay limp in her hands. Nikka forgot everything else and held the little girl to her ear. The helicopter descended through the portal, and its sound cut off abruptly, leaving silence ringing in her ears.

Now she could hear the faint hum of Tierza's heart, and she breathed a relieved sigh. But the faerie wasn't safe yet. Nikka's felt sick with worry and she cradled the sleeping...the dying little girl in her hands. Her eyes stung and she blinked away tears.

Something darted by with a faint chirp. It landed on the branch of a nearby tree, and she squinted at it. A tiny ball of yellow—no bigger than a pea—but it was a perfect little bird.

She looked around with wide eyes. A deer just eight inches tall bounded through the forest. Apples the size of grapes hung from a tree that barely reached her shoulder.

It was just like her world, but on a smaller scale. Incredible. Now she had some idea of what Tierza felt like among the humans. Except in this world Nikka was a powerful giant, even if she was terribly out of place. Down there, Tierza was tiny, helpless, and just as out of place. No wonder she'd been so terrified of everything. Nikka wasn't afraid, but the faeries' world was both familiar and completely different at the same time, an incongruity that was profoundly disturbing.

Tierza twitched and started coughing. It was a deep, rasping cough, and when she licked her lips, her saliva was stained with blood.

Nikka knelt and laid Tierza on the grass, hunching over her. "Hey," she said in a soft voice. "Tierza, we're in your world. You're home. Please wake up."

The little girl didn't respond. Her eyes remained closed and she continued to cough and squirm. Nikka looked up at the blue sky, as if the answers to her questions would be written there. But they weren't. She was so powerful in this world of small people, yet so powerless to help Tierza.

She jumped when the harsh roar of the helicopter shattered the silence of the peaceful landscape. She picked up Tierza and turned to see the chopper rising from the ground.

Then there was a loud snap and it lurched to the side. The blades struck the ground and broke off, sending pieces whirling through the air for hundreds of feet. Then the helicopter fell.

Nikka started running, her heart racing in time with the pounding of her feet. Silence descended over the land again; the helicopter was gone now. Who had been in it? Rod and Jase? Were they even now smashing into the bay and sinking to their deaths?

She swallowed an awful lump in her throat and then reached the top of a small rise near the portal.

The back half of the helicopter protruded from the ground, as if the whole area had turned to quicksand for a moment and swallowed the front. Nikka stopped and stared as her brother crawled out of the wreckage.

"Jason!" she shouted, running forward again. "Where's Dad?"

He stood up, stumbled a few steps, and fell to his hands and knees. Nikka reached him and lifted him up, supporting him with her free hand around his shoulders.

"Don't know," he mumbled. "What happened? Where's Dad?"

"That's what I'm asking you," she said.

"I don't know! He's not here."

Josiah swooped down and landed on the ground nearby. "I'm sorry," he said, holding his chest as he wheezed. "Couldn't keep it open."

"You tried," Nikka said. "What happened?"

"It started closing and the helicopter went out of control. Then the portal closed all the way and cut it in half. The other part will fall to the ground in your world."

Nikka shuddered and tried not to think of her father falling with it.

"How is Jera?"

Nikka looked at the miniature girl in her right hand and stooped a little so Jase could get his arm over her shoulders.

"She's not doing well," Nikka said.

Josiah flew up and landed on her shoulder. He gripped her hair and stared in silence at his daughter.

They moved away from the portal and sat down, facing the wrecked helicopter. Nikka laid Tierza on the ground and Josiah landed beside her.

"Dad didn't make it," Jase said. He curled his arm and stretched his neck to look at his elbow. Then he moistened his fingers in his mouth and rubbed them over the dirty cuts and scrapes on his arms. He seemed a little less shaken now.

"So he...fell?" Nikka asked, and winced. She sounded like a frightened little girl.

"Maybe he had a parachute."

"We're stuck here," she said, beginning to tremble. "How will we get back without...without..."

Jase hugged her. "I'm scared too," he said.

She swallowed. He was her little brother, and even if he was going to learn to fill a man's shoes, he'd still look up to her. She took a deep breath and nodded.

"We'll figure something out," she said.

Jase stood up on unsteady legs and turned away from the broken helicopter. "Can you find out if Dad is okay?" he asked Josiah.

The faerie man looked up from Tierza's motionless body. "Yes, I—"

He cocked his head to the side and listened. Nikka shivered, and then she heard the shouting and sounds of battle. Jase clung to her arm.

Josiah went pale. "They've overrun the capitol, if they're this far! Our forces will be almost gone. My son..."

Nikka held up her brother. "Come on, Jase. We came here to help. Dad most likely fell, with or without a parachute, and nothing we can do will change what happened to him."

Jase nodded, his lips pressed into a thin line.

"Follow me," Josiah said.

Nikka hid Tierza under a small bush at the rim of the portal, and then they ran along as Josiah streaked through the air toward the battle. The faerie drew a short knife from his belt. The siblings gripped their tennis rackets.

"Stick together," Nikka told her brother. "I'll watch your back, you watch mine."

"Mhmm," Jase grunted.

They didn't speak for a moment.

"Tierza is almost dead, isn't she?" Nikka asked, directing the question at Josiah.

"Yes," he replied in a strained voice. "Sometimes the poison works a little faster. Especially in girls."

Just a moment later, they rounded the corner of a cliff about ten feet high and came upon a roiling battlefield. Faeries grappled in the air, fought hand to hand on the ground, and their small dead bodies littered the field. Feathers and blood were everywhere, sticking to faces and clothes.

There were two forces, easy to tell apart. A ragged, motley army led by soldiers dressed mostly in gold fought against a well-organized band of large, silver-winged men. The silver-wings kept their ranks tight, fighting with almost mechanical precision.

"Attack the silver ones," Josiah shouted, and then he shot forward into the melee with a cry of, "For the king! For Jera! For Prince Faray!"

"What do we do?" Jase asked. His voice was surprisingly steady.

"Scare them," Nikka said, putting on her safety glasses. "Do whatever you can. I hate to say it, but we might have to kill some of them."

"I'm ready."

The giants advanced. Allies and enemies alike fled from the two humans, who shouted and roared and swatted the silver-winged attackers with little heed for their thin, six-inch-long swords.

Jase got pricked in the arm, and it only made him angry. He smacked the owner of the sword away, and the stunned faerie fell to the ground with his head at a strange angle. He didn't get back up.

It wasn't long before the silver-wings turned and fled. Nikka and Jase stopped and watched them go, pressing their fingers to their deepest cuts. Their injuries weren't serious, just stabs and slices from the thin, sharp blades that were able to pierce the leather jackets in some places.

Josiah landed on Nikka's shoulder, panting and dripping with sweat. "They're going for reinforcements," he said. "The capitol is in that direction. They would have left a division there to secure the city."

An older faerie man landed on the ground in front of them and looked up. "Josiah Aileron, who do we thank for these timely and very unexpected reinforcements? And how in the name of all Ludic did two humans get here?"

"You have my daughter to thank, Hector," Josiah said. "And she lies dying not far from here."

The other faerie stared up at Nikka. She noted that he stood straight and tall like an old, experienced general.

"You are friends of Jera Aileron?" he asked.

"Yes," Jase said, stooping down with a scowl. "Are you one of the creatures who poisoned her?"

Hector took a step back. "I didn't have any choice."

"There's no cure, is there?"

"Actually..."

Josiah flew down and landed beside him. "What? Are you saying there is?"

"It was discovered recently. A very rare substance that counteracts the effects of the venom. Only one small bottle of it exists right now."

Jase jumped to his feet. "Where is it?"

"In the king's chamber, locked up."

"In the capitol, of course," Nikka sighed.

"Then let's go!" Jase shouted.

His sister caught his arm. "Wait," she said. "Just...wait a minute."

"You go back and get Jera," Hector said. "I will retrieve the cure. I can fly much faster than you humans can run."

"What about the enemy?" Josiah said. "They must have the city by now."

"They do. But I know of tunnels underneath. I should be able to get in and out unnoticed."

"I'm coming with you," Josiah said.

"No, stay with your daughter. If she is dying, these may be the last minutes you have with her, as much as I hate to say it. I will take a few of the strongest guards with me."

Nikka turned around and saw that the whole army was gathered together, staring up in silence at the humans. She gave them a little wave and said, "Hi..."

Josiah landed on her shoulder again, and Hector darted over to the army. He picked out a dozen stout faeries who weren't seriously injured and flew away in the same direction the silver-wings had retreated.

Jase grabbed Nikka's hand. "Come on. Let's get Tierza."

"She doesn't have much time," Josiah said. "We should get her and come back to meet Hector along the way, as close to the city as we can."

They left the army behind and ran back toward the portal. When they got there, they almost thought Tierza was dead already. But Nikka picked her up and she stirred a little, and that was enough to give them hope. They turned around and started running again.

Nikka's legs began to feel heavier. Jase's breathing grew faster, and he grabbed his side with a wince. Josiah flew out ahead of them in impatient short bursts of speed that made him look like a large songbird.

They passed the battlefield again and kept going. Nikka looked closely at the little houses they came across, and in some of them she could see tiny faces peering out the windows. Faerie children, who were no doubt wondering where the wingless giants came from.

Finally Nikka had to stop. When she did, Jase sat down hard and then flopped onto his back, gasping for air. She sat beside him and held Tierza up close to her face. The little girl was shaking, still unconscious.

"I see someone!" Josiah shouted, diving down from the sky. "I think Hector is coming."

Nikka laid Tierza on the ground and Josiah landed beside her. The little girl stretched out her arms, like she was fending off an invisible assailant. Her face was ghostly white, her green eyes wide and dull, unseeing. She stiffened, grasping at the air, her mouth open but silent.

Nikka watched and massaged a cramp out of her side, still trying to catch her breath.

Hector flew down and crash-landed beside Tierza. Blood covered his clothes from several deep gashes, and he held out a small bottle before slumping over.

"What happened to the others?" Josiah asked.

"Gone," Hector gasped. "All...dead. I'm the only one who got out..." He trailed off and became very still.

Josiah grabbed his friend's hand. "Hector?"

There was no reply.

He took the bottle and twisted off the cap with shaking hands, and at that moment Tierza convulsed one last time and her arms went limp. Her mouth closed. Her chest fell with her last breath. Then she stopped moving completely.

Chapter Nineteen

Life and Death

"She's dead," Josiah cried, pressing his hand to the side of Tierza's throat. "It's too late!"

"Give her the cure anyway," Jase shouted as he sat up. "And pray for a miracle."

Josiah poured the cure down his daughter's throat, and then dropped the bottle and turned away, covering his face with his hands and sobbing.

Jase picked up Tierza and held her flat across both of his hands, watching closely for any sign of life. Tears blurred his vision and he blinked them away furiously.

"Come back, Tierza," he muttered. "Come back..."

Josiah crawled to Hector's side and felt his throat. Then he sat back on his heels with a groan.

"What?" Nikka asked.

"He's...dead." Josiah stood and grabbed handfuls of his hair, tilting his head back to holler his anger and grief at the sky. Then he slouched and staggered a short distance away, flapping his wings erratically to keep his balance.

Jase still stared at Tierza, wishing his gaze could put life back into her. She hadn't moved at all. Not a single breath.

"She's dead, Jase," Nikka said, putting her hands gently on his shoulders.

He gritted his teeth and began to cry. He fell to his knees, and Tierza's body almost bounced out of his hands. He curled his fingers around her.

"Please," he moaned. And it was all he could think to say.

Nikka knelt beside him and laid her cheek on the top of his head. She hugged him and he relaxed a little.

"Maybe she has wings again," Nikka whispered.

"Do faeries go to heaven?" Jase asked.

"I'm sure they do. Tierza was as much a person as you."

"Will we see her again?"

Nikka kissed her brother's head. "I hope so. Probably."

He lowered his hands to lay the little girl on the ground, and tears spilled down his cheeks. But then he felt something brush his thumb.

"Nikka!" he said. His voice sounded almost frightened.

She patted his shoulder. "We'll be all right."

Jase blinked and peered at his hands. Tierza had moved her left arm.

"Nikka, she moved."

"What?" His sister straightened up and leaned forward. "Are you imagining it?"

"No! Honest, I'm not. She moved her arm. There she goes again!"

Josiah came streaking back and made an awkward crash landing on the ground in front of them. "What's going on?" he demanded.

Jase ignored everyone else, fixing all his attention on Tierza. Yes, she had moved. First her left arm, then her right. Tiny, almost imperceptible twitches.

A couple minutes passed, and nobody said anything. They all watched Tierza, hardly breathing. The little girl was definitely alive. Her chest began moving up and down as she breathed, her fingers clenched into fists, and then all of a sudden she started kicking and fighting and screaming.

"Tierza, you're all right!" Jase said. "Calm down, you're safe."

After a moment she went limp again. Now her chest was heaving and she was drenched with sweat. Her skin had regained more color than Jase could ever remember it having.

Then she opened her eyes, squinting in the sunlight. "Father?" she mumbled.

Jase sat down and held her close to the ground so Josiah could reach her.

"I'm here, Jera," Josiah said. He leaned over and hugged her, lifting her head and shoulders off Jase's hands.

"I thought I died," she said. Her voice was weak, the words slurred.

"I thought so too, but you're still here. There was a cure, Jera. Hector got it for you. He died for you."

Tierza wasn't very lucid yet. "Oh..." she mumbled. "Don't let me die..."

Josiah clung to her, trembling as he wept silently. "No, I won't. I won't, darling."

Jase set Tierza in her father's arms and leaned against Nikka's shoulder. He suddenly felt exhausted. But he remembered something else that had almost been forgotten in the urgent moment.

"Dad!" Jase cried. "Nikka, we've got to get home. Somehow. We need parachutes. I'm so tired though, and—"

"Calm down," she said. "We'll figure it out."

Josiah looked up at them with Tierza curled up in his arms like a small child. "What about the silver invaders?" he asked. "They aren't gone yet. Can you still help?"

"Of course we can," Nikka said. Then she sighed. "I'm tired too, Jason. But we have one last battle to fight."

Jase staggered to his feet and then helped his sister up. "Okay, I think I can handle that. Mister Aileron, you hang on to your little girl. Leave the heroic stuff to us. We'll be back...sometime."

"Can you find the city?" Josiah asked.

Nikka looked in the direction of the capitol and shaded her eyes. "Can we? I can see it from here."

"Good luck, then. I'm sure you will be fine."

They left Tierza and her father and jogged toward the city. It was about half a mile away, about three miles in faerie terms.

"Never thought we'd be fighting an entire army," Nikka said.

"I never thought we'd *be* an entire army," Jase puffed.

Nikka gave a dry chuckle. "Do you think we can handle this on our own?"

"For sure. I'll bet those faerie punks will get up and fly when they see us coming."

"Maybe they're already gone. Who wants to face two angry giants?"

Jase scowled. "This giant is even angrier than before."

Nikka patted his shoulder. "Just don't let anger cloud your mind."

They stopped talking when they neared the city. The buildings were small on the outskirts, most no higher than three feet—which was two levels. The streets were only three or four feet wide, sometimes even narrower, so Nikka and Jase went single file. Nikka in front.

The place seemed to be deserted. Everyone had either fled or gone into hiding. Jase hoped that included the silver-wings.

But then they came to the magnificent capitol building, a domed structure over twenty feet high, with dozens of fancy little balconies. They peered over the five-foot-high wall into the courtyard, and saw that it was packed with what must have been the full remaining force of the silver-winged invaders.

Nikka jerked back and dragged Jase with her.

"They've seen us already," he said.

"And they intend to fight again," she added.

He eyed the gate. "You still remember how to do those karate kicks?"

A moment later the gate tore loose from its hinges and fell into the courtyard, pinning an entire regiment of the enemy beneath it. The rest had raised their weapons in anticipation of attacking, but seeing Nikka standing tall in the gate with her fists on her hips, they drew back in fear.

"Charge, you cowards!" one in the very back yelled.

"Stay where you are," Nikka ordered. Her voice was loud and menacing, and the enemy's forces didn't move.

"We aren't here to crush you," she continued. "But you aren't welcome here either. You have a chance to go back to wherever you came from. Do that, or you'll deal with me and my brother."

Almost half of the army took to the sky and streaked away to the east, and the ones they left behind started to advance, some casting angry glances at their fleeing friends.

"They're the smart ones," Nikka said, gesturing at the silvery runaways that glinted in the sun. She lifted the gate, letting the trapped faeries loose. Most of them flew away, except for a few with broken wings that crawled into the corners.

Jase stepped up beside his sister and they strode into the courtyard. Nikka didn't bother to stoop under the gateway arch, instead choosing to strike the relatively thin column of mortared stones with her palm. It shattered and sent chunks raining over the faeries inside.

Another regiment took to the sky. The rest began to look uneasy.

"Yep, a flashy entrance sure helps," Jase said with a smirk, not quite loud enough for his sister to hear.

Then he stepped forward, making exaggerated stomping motions. He couldn't bring himself to actually crush any of them, no matter how villainous they were. They were still faeries, still little people.

The remaining army launched themselves at the giants, swinging their little swords and spears. Some of them even threw what looked like firecrackers, which did no more than startle Jase and give him a few minor burns. He stood with his back against Nikka's, and they swung their tennis rackets this way and that, as if they were fighting a swarm of very large bees.

There were still enough of the enemy to make it a tough fight. Jase got stabbed in the hand and dropped his racket. He snatched two faeries from the air in front of his face and smashed their little heads together, dropping their limp bodies with a shudder. Then he snatched up the racket again and kept swinging.

This was so different from what he'd imagined when he first thought of coming here. He had rushed into the adventure thinking about the glory of defeating a murderous enemy. Now that he was in the middle of it all, as one of the only significant forces that stood between these attackers and their weakened prey, he realized that he only still fought because it was right. He hated hurting them. He hated the idea that doing so could bring him fame.

But it was the right thing to do, wasn't it? Josiah was right—if the strong didn't risk themselves in battle, the weak might die afterward.

After a few minutes Jase's arms were crisscrossed with shallow cuts, which stung but didn't bleed enough to be harmful. The sleeves of his leather jacket hung in tatters, and he was glad it wasn't his own skin. The attacking faeries dwindled, and injured ones littered the ground. Finally the silver-wings left off the attack and rose into the sky like a flock of angry birds.

"Get out of the country!" Nikka shouted, shaking her bloody fists over her head. "Don't come back or we'll have to deal with you!"

The remainder of the enemy that was able to fly streaked away. They didn't need any more proof that they were beaten.

"We did it," Jase said, staring up into the sky. "You were awesome, Nikka."

She put her arm around his shoulders. "So were you."

"We make a great two-person army."

Nikka laughed and ruffled his hair, and then he laughed, and they kept laughing, releasing the tension as they made their way out of the city at a relaxed pace.

The sun was sinking below the horizon when they arrived at the army's little camp, not far from where they'd won their first battle. The faeries' tents were tiny, hardly ten inches tall, except for one large one that stood almost two feet high at the center pole. That one was at the edge of the camp, and Jase got down on his hands and knees to peer in. The ground inside was covered with cots, where wounded and dying faeries were tended. It looked just like what he imagined an army hospital tent would look like, with nurses and doctors and a lot of bandages. There was no magic in use here, it seemed.

A young faerie lady in an apron was the first to see him. She let out a hair-raising scream and scrambled behind a pile of blankets. Others either froze or tried to hide, some silently and some with squeaks of fright.

"Don't be afraid," Jase said. "We just sent those silver-winged jerks running home to their mommies. Your city is safe again."

No one responded, until Josiah walked in the other side of the tent and looked up at the huge face.

"It's all right," he said, helping a terrified girl up. "They're on our side."

The medical staff went back to their business, though they continued to cast distrustful glances at the huge intruder.

Josiah crossed the room and stopped by a cot not far from Jase. Tierza lay there, sound asleep and breathing fine. Satisfied, Josiah stepped out the back of the tent and looked up at Jase and Nikka.

"I'm sorry that most of my people won't welcome you, despite what you've done. You really deserve better."

"It's okay," Jase said. "I understand. We're as tall as trees here. I'd be afraid if I was in your place."

Josiah managed a small smile. "We can hardly repay you. You've both been very brave, and you've done far more than you had to."

"If you can get us home," Nikka said, "that's good enough for us."

"I've been thinking about that. The portal opens by itself at sunrise and sunset, and stays open for almost half an hour. Sunset is already past, but at dawn we can tie a long rope to a tree and let you down. If we can get a rope long enough."

Jase patted his stomach. "I don't know how well I'd do with that. Heights, and climbing...I think I'd get sick." He looked at the tent, and then poked the side of it. "Do you have a lot of material like this?"

Josiah frowned. "We have some at the farm that we use for covering crops that need to stay dry or warm. But how would that help?"

Jase smiled. "I need two squares of it, as big as you have, and a lot of rope."

"If you insist. I'll get that here as soon as I can."

"We'll probably have to postpone our trip down until later in the day so I can make our parachutes. But you won't have to keep the portal open for long. Just enough time for us to jump through."

Josiah looked a little pale at the mention of jumping through. "As you wish," he muttered. "I hope you'll be all right."

As twilight wore on, Jase and Nikka washed their injuries in the fresh, clear water of a nearby lake. The faeries didn't have enough clean material for bandaging, but the cuts were already healing well so they left them uncovered.

"That's going to be a lot of little scars," Jase said, examining his arm.

Nikka flicked away her last redfruit stem and lay back on the grass with a sigh. "Have you ever had better fruit?" she asked.

"Nope. Those red ones tasted a lot like bananas, did you notice?"

"No wonder Tierza...er, Jera likes bananas so much. Her dad said the red ones are her favorite food."

"It'll be hard to call her Jera," Jase murmured.

"It'll be even harder to leave her behind and go home."

"I wish we could stay here, at least for a little while."

Nikka sighed. "We don't belong here. They're all afraid of us, except Josiah and T...Jera."

"I know. You don't think she'll go back down there with us?"

"She has a family here, Jason. Don't you think she'll want to be with her family?"

He shrugged. "We could ask her."

"No. Let her make her own choice. I doubt she'll want to leave this world again."

Jase folded his hands behind his head and fixed his gaze on the stars. They weren't like the stars in the sky back at home. These ones came in all colors, and they twinkled boldly like Christmas lights.

"I really love this place," Jase muttered. "Too bad I can't shrink myself so I'd fit in."

And then he rolled onto his side and fell asleep.

Chapter Twenty

Where Home Is

Jase awoke just before dawn. He scooted away from his sleeping sister and stood up, stretching his arms and yawning.

The faerie camp was already awake. He smelled the distinctive odor of baking bread, which was probably the same in every world. On the ground nearby lay two large rolls of fabric. It must have taken at least a couple dozen faeries to move each one. A few coils of rope sat beside them. About a quarter inch wide, and when he picked up an end of it, he was surprised at how silky it felt. He tested its strength by biting and yanking on the end. None of the strands broke, and he nodded in satisfaction.

Nikka got up with the sun, a few minutes later, and they sat side by side for a short time and soaked up the first warm rays.

"It's Sunday," Jase said.

"Hmm," Nikka murmured. She had her eyes closed and her face turned toward the sun.

"Do you think Mom is worried about us?"

"Very worried," Nikka said.

"And Dad?"

"He never worries. Not much, at least. He's too optimistic."

Jase stood, using her shoulder to push himself up. "I'm going to see if Jera is awake."

He walked to the camp and peered into the hospital tent again. And he smiled when he saw the little girl sitting up on her cot.

"Hey, Jera," he said, keeping his voice low so he wouldn't wake up the sleeping patients.

She blinked at him and yawned. "Jase? You're here?"

"How do you feel?"

She stood up and walked toward him. She seemed steady enough.

"I feel all right," she said.

He picked her up when she reached him and she sat on his hand with her arms wrapped around his thumb.

"I'm going home today," he said.

"That's good."

She sounded glum. Jase raised her to the level of his eyes, and she turned her face to avoid his gaze.

"Is something wrong?" he asked.

Jera made an effort to smile. "No. I'm just thinking."

"Oh. You sound depressed."

"I'm tired."

"Then I suppose you should sleep." He stooped back down and set her outside the tent.

"Jase?"

"Yeah?"

She stared down at her feet and shifted them a little. Then she turned and went inside.

For the next few hours Jase could barely think of anything other than Jera. He worked on the parachutes with Nikka's help, designing them from his memory of the one he'd made with his father a couple years ago. They folded the edges of the material back multiple times, and then sewed circles in them with needles made out of broken blades from the army, and thread that was actually thin rope like the cords the faeries used to anchor their tents. Using his pocketknife, Jase cut holes in the middle of each sewn circle.

After they had the eyelets made all around the edges of both parachutes, which took until mid-afternoon, they threaded hundreds of feet of the big rope through, doubling it up all around for extra strength. They tied all the bottom ends to a couple sticks—or logs, as the faeries called them.

While Nikka was threading rope, Jase ran back to the helicopter wreck. The faeries had managed to haul it out before the portal opened at sunset and dropped the rest of the helicopter into the bay. Jase retrieved a couple safety harness pieces and some good hefty rope from the emergency kit. He hoped that since there was no parachute in this half of the wreck, it meant that his dad had gotten it. He knew there was an emergency one in the helicopter before the crash.

With the materials from the wreck he improvised a couple harnesses, drawing on his good knowledge of knots. He wasn't a Boy Scout yet, but he would be soon. And when he was, he wanted to make an impression by knowing as much as he could. It sure was useful to know these knots.

By early evening the harnesses were tied to the parachutes, and Jase cut a vent in the middle of each. They looked quite inviting.

"I don't know if I can trust this contraption," Nikka said as they stood there admiring their work.

They looked inviting to Jase. He was proud of their work. These were some good parachutes, he thought. Overlooking the mess of knots and ropes.

They hadn't seen Jera all day. During his breaks throughout the afternoon, Jase tried to find her, but he wasn't able to. He didn't see Josiah either, and most of the other faeries stayed at a safe distance, watching the giants at work in frightened silence. A few of the braver ones, or the most curious, came close enough to ask what he was making.

For dinner they had a few loaves of faerie bread, which was very sweet, topped with greatfruit, which was even sweeter. The sweetness almost gave Jase a headache.

Josiah found them after they ate. "Are you ready?" he asked.

Jase nodded. "Parachutes are finished, sir. Ready to deploy."

"I'll open the portal for you."

"Can we say goodbye to Jera first?" Nikka asked.

Josiah looked uncomfortable. "I don't know where she is. She wandered off sometime this afternoon."

They rolled up their parachutes slowly, hesitating as they thought of actually leaving. A few minutes later they waved goodbye to the faeries and set out for the portal.

The hike was done in silence, and when they reached the circular depression, Jase dropped his rolled-up parachute on the ground and sat down.

"What's wrong with her?" he grumbled. "Can't she say goodbye to her friends?"

"Who?" a small voice asked.

They turned and saw Jera crawl from behind a bush. "I wanted to be alone for a while," she said.

Josiah flew down from Nikka's shoulder.

"We're leaving tonight," Jase said.

"I know. I guess I'll miss you." She looked up at them and he realized she'd been crying. There were streaks of dried tears on her cheeks.

She must have realized that he'd seen them because she bowed her head again and scrubbed at her cheeks.

Nikka cleared her throat. "We'll see each other again," she said. "I hope. Someday. Just rem..."

She choked up and stopped. Jase thought he knew what she was going to say.

"Remember us," he finished for her. "And stay safe."

Jera nodded, but kept her gaze fixed on the ground.

"I'll go first," Jase said, starting to strap on his harness.

Nikka shook her head. "No, let me."

"What, just because you're older?"

"Maybe because something might go wrong."

"Then I should go, because I'm a man."

She smiled and ran her fingers through his hair, making it stick up. "Maybe you are, but you're still my little brother."

Nikka strapped on her harness and walked to the middle of the portal. She laid the parachute out on the ground behind her and then faced her brother and waved.

"Send me down," she said.

Josiah pressed his hands against the edge of the circle. The ground dissolved from under Nikka's feet and she dropped with a sharp cry. The parachute billowed out above her and filled with air. Jase scrambled to the edge on his hands and knees and looked down, watching his sister float slowly toward the Golden Gate Bridge.

Then the ground appeared again and he stood up.

"My turn," he said, walking out over the portal. "Goodbye, Jera."

"Wait!" she cried. "Jase, watch for me when you get down there. Can you do that? Wait until sunset."

He could only nod.

Then the ground vanished from under him and he dropped through. He couldn't keep in a surprised shriek, but when the parachute caught him he shut his mouth and opened his eyes.

San Francisco spread out before him, sparkling in the slanting late afternoon sun. A breeze caught him and steered him toward the end of the bridge, in the same direction Nikka was going. He saw the car, still parked near the water, and as he got closer, he could see two figures in the front seats.

The children landed in the shallow water a few yards from shore, first Nikka and then Jase just a minute behind her. They waded to dry land and shed the parachutes, and then ran over the grass to the car where their parents waited.

Jera rode to camp on her father's back, nestled between his wings. Her whole family was there. She'd seen them earlier, including Torry who was in the hospital tent with a non-fatal stab wound in his belly.

Her family. She felt strangely detached from them now. But she was at an age when children became adults and left home to start their independent lives. Maybe it was time for her to do that and let her past go.

When they landed, she saw a circle of old faeries sitting in the grass a short distance from the tents. There was a gap in the perfect ring.

"They asked me to take Hector's place on the council," Josiah said.

He led her to the circle and sat down in the gap. She knelt behind him and sat back on her heels.

The Duce stood up, his ancient face sagging. "Who is responsible for bringing to us those two giants, who saved our country from destruction?"

Josiah took his daughter's arm, lifted her to her feet, and propelled her forward. "My daughter, sir. Jera Aileron."

"So I have heard," the Duce muttered. "And she seems to have beaten the venom. Perhaps the justice of fate has found her innocent."

There was a long moment of silence, and Jera stood awkwardly in front of her father. She was sure that she'd made up her mind. Banishment or pardon, she knew where she was going.

"We have come to a decision about you," the Duce said. "Step forward, please."

For the second time in two weeks, she stood before the ancient faerie to hear the cold delivery of his verdict.

"You have saved all of our lives," he said, sounding somewhat reluctant to be admitting they had been wrong about her. "Jera Aileron, as our thanks we offer you a full pardon. You may return home, and your crime is forgotten."

She frowned. "My crime? I never did it, and you know that."

There was another moment of silence, and several of the Court members turned red.

"Either way," the Duce grumbled, "you are forgiven."

She looked around at the assembled faeries, with all their feathery wings gleaming in the sunlight. "What about my wings?" she asked in a low voice.

He sighed. "They have been removed permanently. It cannot be undone."

"Then you removed me permanently. I'm not one of you anymore; you already made me an outcast. I don't think I want to come back."

Her father stood and came forward to kneel before her. "But where will you go?" he asked. "Jera, you have a family here. You're forgiven. Why can't you come home?"

She laid a hand on his shoulder and felt tears sting her eyes. "I don't belong here anymore. All of you made sure of that."

Josiah's face was white. "Jera..."

"Father, you...we do have a family. I still love you all, but you have to let me go. Here everyone has wings, except for the criminals, but I'm not a criminal. I think it's time for me to move on and start a new life."

She stood still. The Court around them was silent, and her heart pounded in her chest.

"Where will you go?" Josiah whispered.

She swallowed. "The humans took care of me."

"You don't belong with them! Just because someone helped you doesn't mean they want you to stick around forever. That's a whole different world down there."

"No, it's mostly the same. Both worlds are filled with people who love and people who hate. People who help and people who abandon you."

"I'm sorry!"

"You poisoned me!" she cried, her voice rising in pitch. "You let them try to kill me and you sent me away. I can't come back, even though I want to."

She stopped, breathing rapidly. She wanted to? Tears stung her eyes and she realized just how much she wanted to go home. Maybe her decision wasn't the best.

Her father stood and laid his hands on her shoulders. "You're grown up," he said. "It's your choice. All I ask is that you forgive me for being a terrible father."

Jera leaned against him, and suddenly she didn't feel grown up anymore. She felt like a little girl again. She wanted her father back. And the only way she could have that would be to forget what he'd done.

"I forgive you," she whispered, with some effort. But once she said it, she felt sudden relief. It didn't matter anymore. The pain was over. She could go home.

"Thank you," Josiah said, his voice low. He wrapped his arms tightly around her. "I really don't deserve that, but I hope I'll never have to beg your forgiveness again. I hope I've learned something from this that I'll never forget."

When he relaxed and she stepped out of his embrace, she noticed that the circle of the Court wasn't there anymore. They were all walking back to the camp.

"I can hardly understand how you could forgive me after that," he said, keeping his head bowed.

"Father." She put her hand under his chin and made him look at her. Just like Faray had done to her. "I'm alive, and I'm not dying. I—"

Josiah winced. "Your wings, Jera."

She was silent for a moment. Then she spoke in a very soft voice. "That wasn't your fault. It wasn't even the Court's fault. The king ordered it."

"But a moment ago—"

"I was angry. I'm sorry."

"Oh, Jera, you don't need to be sorry. Not at all." He sounded anguished and tears spilled down his cheeks.

She shrugged.

"Really. You were the victim. It's nothing to apologize for." He rubbed his eyes. "Will you come home?"

"Yes, I will."

"And you'll stay?"

"For a while."

"I hope you stay until you find a good man and leave to be a wonderful mother."

She smiled. "I hope so too."

"I can just see you with a young man, flying together..." He trailed off with a pained look. "Oh, I'm sorry..."

Jera sighed and looked up at the sky. Yes, she would miss flying. But there were more important things in life. Her heart could find another way to soar.

"Don't worry about it," she said.

Josiah held her hand. "Shall we go home?"

"Not yet. There's something else I have to do first." Jera squinted at the setting sun. "It won't take long, but I need a ride."

Rod and Rayna could barely comprehend what was happening when their children flung the car doors open and shook them awake. Two sopping wet and laughing kids, jabbering about falling from the sky? Confusing, even for people who hadn't just woken up.

"Let me get this straight," Rod said as he climbed out of the car. "You remembered how to build a parachute, and made one for each of you so you could get down here?"

"That's right," Jase said, giving his dad a hug. "Aren't you proud of me?"

Rod looked over the car's roof at Rayna, and she smiled as she embraced Nikka. "Yes, Jason, very proud."

A few minutes later they were all seated in the grass, and Jase and Nikka told in detail about how they'd chased off an entire army of faeries. They described the world vividly, all the colorful stars and the fruit and especially the faeries with their beautiful wings. Rod said he wanted to visit, and for once Rayna didn't argue with him.

"I know, but we wouldn't fit in," Jase said. He turned and looked up at the spot in the sky where the portal was. "I wanted to stay there too, but we belong down here."

Rod ruffled his son's hair. "I think you're right, little man."

The conversation continued, but Jase didn't say anything more. He kept his gaze on the sky, waiting for sunset with a sick feeling in his stomach.

A few more minutes passed, and then the sun shone through a gap in the clouds, flooding the entire area with light. The red on the bridge turned to a brilliant shimmering gold, and Jase's eyes widened.

The bridge. It's all golden. Can't you see? It's bright gold and sparkly.

Maybe it was because he'd spent time in the faeries' world that he now saw things only they could see. He glanced at his family. Nikka was also staring at the bridge, but his parents didn't seem to notice.

He turned back, and then he noticed the small, winged figure flying down toward them.

Jera rode on her father's back all the way to the ground, and when she climbed off he turned and gave her a hug.

"I love you," he whispered in her ear.

She smiled and looked up to see Jase come running over the grass.

"Jera!" he shouted. "What happened up there?"

"They pardoned me for a crime I never committed."

Nikka, Rayna, and Rod stopped behind Jase. The boy picked her up and spoke in a whisper. "So what happens now?"

"I want to go home."

He looked up into the sky. "Isn't your home...there?"

Jera followed his gaze. "Yes," she said.

He didn't say anything, and she looked at him to see tears in his eyes.

"Don't cry," she said, trying to smile. "We can visit sometimes. It's not like I'm dying now."

Jase wiped his eyes and nodded. "Of course."

Nikka put her arm around her brother's shoulders. "We'll miss you anyway, Jera. You're a very nice little person."

"And you..." Jera could barely speak—now *she* was starting to cry. "Thank you for everything. You're real heroes, you know."

Josiah flew up and landed on Nikka's shoulder. "The Ludic may have feared you," he said, "but you will live on in their fireside stories for a long time."

Nikka blushed a little.

"It was exciting," Jase said. "Scary, tiring, and painful, but I'd do it all over again. Just to have more time in that charming world of yours."

Jera sat up straight in Jase's hands and leaned over to look at Rod and Rayna, who stood behind their children. Jase and Nikka turned around.

"It was a pleasure meeting you both," Rod said, looking from Jera to her father. "And don't worry about the helicopter. I have insurance."

"Nice to meet you too," the little girl said with a smile.

Jase sat down and set Jera on the ground. She stood up straight and Josiah landed beside her.

"What about your wings?" Jase asked. "You don't get them back?"

She tried not to look sad, but Jase's expression told her he noticed. "No. But I'll be fine. I'm alive, right? I can survive without wings."

"What you need," Rod said, "is a little helicopter."

Jase laughed. "That would be great."

Jera felt her father's hand on her shoulder and she glanced at him. "I think...I'm going home now," she said.

Silence. She gazed up at the humans, and bit her lip as she tried not to cry. "Goodbye," she whispered.

Then she climbed onto her father's back and he launched into the air. Jase waved and shouted goodbye over and over again. She watched him and his family get smaller and smaller behind her, until the world changed.

Jera took a deep breath of the fresh summer air in her homeland and laid her cheek on the back of Josiah's head. She listened to the rush of the wind, and the swishing of his feathers through the air. A little thrill went through her and she shivered. It had been a very long time since she rode on her father's back. She loved it.

"I think your mother made pie tonight," Josiah said.

Jera smiled and closed her eyes.

"There are plenty of berries to pick," he continued. "And someone needs to teach the baby to fly. She keeps crashing into walls."

The End

A hardcover version of this book can
be purchased at
www.lulu.com/spotlight/luke_alistar

About the Author

Luke Alistar works magic with his copious words in every genre he feels like writing. He also plays the piano, writes music, composes songs, and does various other artistic things. He loves hats, knives, swords, books, music by Chopin, country music, and Porsches. He is the author of _The Unseen_, the Offset Trilogy, and _The Element of Surprise_, a collection of comical stories. _Velvet's Wings_ is his first children's book.

Find him online at www.LukeAlistar.com or www.mindwielders.com

About the Illustrator

Stephen Lauser once entered an art contest with three drawings, and took home the first, second, and third place ribbons. He sells his art to whoever wants to buy it and illustrates his own books and those of his brothers. At age sixteen, he is learning how to do 3D modeling and animation on the computer and would like to someday make a career of it. He has studied art under a professional illustrator for a few years and has an impressive portfolio.

Made in the USA
San Bernardino, CA
12 May 2014